DARK SECRETS

RICHARD GERBER

Published by

RG Livre Publisher
2021

Book cover design and formatting services by SelfPublishingLab.com

ISBN:
978-1-7372249-0-7 (pbk)

This book is dedicated to Police Officer Joseph Mantegna, badge 464, who helped to keep Baltimore City and its harbor safe during his 25-year career with the Baltimore Police Department, April 19, 1971 to May 1, 1996. He was a dear close friend, whose untimely death on May 3, 2010, sadden everyone who knew him. He is the inspiration for the character of the same name in this novel. Rest in peace, Joe.

Contents

The Beginning

1976

1

Baltimore City, Maryland
June 1976

Twenty-three-year-old Nick Witkowski and his partner were the second car to arrive. His partner jumped out first. Tall, five feet eleven inches, and thin, Rich Ward was nimble. Witkowski was shorter, five feet and eight inches, and slightly overweight. Hurrying to get from behind the wheel he yelled at Ward, "You forgot your flashlight." Ward went back to the car as Witkowski walked towards two other officers standing by their car twenty feet away. They had received a call to back up O'Brien and Lewandowski at eight-thirty P.M.

"Youze guys check around here. Don't go into any buildings 'til back-up comes. I'm going across the street," Larry O'Brien commanded. He had one stripe, so he led. The others were slick sleeves.

"How soon for more back-up?" Bert Lewandowski asked.

"Dispatch said maybe fifteen minutes. It's a busy evening," O'Brien explained.

Ward looked up and scanned the building fronts. "I don't like this one bit. Too many hiding spots, like for a sniper."

"Be careful and try not to shoot a squatter or homeless person," O'Brien warned.

Lewandowski pointed north at one of the abandoned buildings and said, "I saw a wino over there. I hope he stays away from us."

"The winos and bums should be gone by now. They don't stick around when they see cops," Ward said.

On a tip, a twenty-two-year-old wanted suspect, one William Brocius, aka C. Bill, had been spotted lurking down by the waterfront on Pratt Street. Witkowski and the others were sent to check it out. It was nine thirty in the evening and they had their flashlights aimed at the broken windows of abandoned warehouses slated for demolition. Ward wasn't the only one feeling antsy, the area gave Witkowski a prickly sensation. Urban renewal couldn't come fast enough for him. Two piers to the west, Witkowski looked at the almost completed World Trade Center at the end of the harbor. Dead fish, oil and diesel fumes breezed by him from the inner harbor to remind him that the renewal had a long way to go.

On the harbor side of Pratt Street Officer O'Brien hollered, "Over here guys, I think I saw someone run into the Pier Four Power Plant."

O'Brien had yelled from Pier 4 where, since nineteen seventy-three, the abandoned Baltimore Gas and Electric power plant stood. Pier 4 was one of the five different names the power plant was known as. Unfortunately, it presented itself as an excellent trap, no matter what anyone called it.

Lewandowski and Ward drew their service revolvers and sprinted across the nearly deserted Pratt Street and joined O'Brien who had been approaching the site cautiously.

Witkowski slowly crossed Pratt, and then he pulled his four-inch barreled weapon. His eyes scanned up and down the street. He worried about the suspect getting away.

Witkowski maneuvered around trash, broken glass, discarded tires, chunks of metal, and other debris—normal for this part of the city. His footsteps crunched on the pavement scattering the rats that scurried around him. Witkowski's flashlight bobbed and scanned in front of him exploring the darkness.

The empty Pier 4 Power Plant, with its multiple dark eyes, leered down on them, mocking: I'm watching you. Witkowski moved carefully with the others near him. He thought they all looked like the Earp's and Doc Holliday in Tombstone—four abreast, with him off to the left side, three feet behind them. The rotten smells coming off the harbor, mixed with the odors of the vandalized empty warehouses made his stomach queasy. *This city stinks.* McCormick Spice Company nearby couldn't mask the rancid odor.

Remembering what happened to five of his brother officers on Good Friday two months before, Witkowski's senses were heightened. One officer was killed and four others were critically wounded by an eighteen-year-old sniper. It happened just one block north and around twenty blocks west. The guy they were after was a twenty-two-year-old murderer, a cold-blooded killer. Nick hoped he wouldn't try to snipe them.

Wiping his eyes with his bare left arm, holding his revolver stretched out with his right arm. Hot, humid and, still over ninety degrees, streams of sweat trickled down into Nick's eyes. Witkowski squinted, thought he saw something and aimed his light at it.

"Over there!" Witkowski shouted as his flashlight beam caught a phantom darting across a doorway.

Witkowski happened to be last as they ran towards the door in the power plant where the image had been. They were ambushed by the suspect charging out of the building firing his pistols, disorientating them with muzzle flashes and loud reports.

Larry O'Brien stopped, looked up slightly and collapsed on his back—a hole in his forehead. Rich Ward, three feet in front of and off to Witkowski's right side suddenly pitched forward and crumpled to the ground. Bert Lewandowski fired a shot that missed the suspect, then he too hit the cement lot and died.

In the few street lights that worked, Witkowski watched as the man came at him. Instinctively he dropped into a crouch and everything slowed down. Two handed, Nick pointed his revolver at the suspect and fired at the same time the shooter did. Nick twisted when a bullet struck him in the left arm and felt a burn in his side. It was hard to see his target in the dim light, coupled with gun flashes and the suspect zig zagging. He fired his revolver again, staggering when he thought he slipped on something. His leg collapsed under him and he hit the debris filled concrete hard.

No sound except…footfalls running close towards him. The wanted murderer fired his gun at Witkowski as he ran by. Bits of concrete peppered the side of his face. The dark figure growing smaller as it retreated away from him into the night.

Nick Witkowski didn't know he was the last one shot as he laid in his pool of blood. Its stickiness made him more uncomfortable and seemed to glue him to the pavement. The strong copper and gunpowder odor wafted unpleasantly into his nostrils until a breeze carried it away. He had fallen on his back and his eyes pointed up at the starless night sky, drowned out by the city's lights. He moved his leg and winced. Hit three times, in the side, arm, and leg, he knew he couldn't help arresting the suspect. The three other officers…where were they? He lay there in a daze for a minute or two before comprehending what had just happened. He could only move his head a little and could not see much except the smoke stacks of the power plant and the dark sky.

As he laid there, various thoughts swirled through his mind. The physical pain tormented him as he thought about what went wrong. Maybe they shouldn't have been so close together. He felt stupid for charging into the doorway instead of being cautious. An old cop and robber movie popped into his head reminding him of how the cop ran around a corner, with gun in hand, and met death. *How dumb. Fine for the movies, not real police work. Should have done it better.*

A distant ship's horn sounded. He didn't hear the other officers. Were they alive or had they chased the suspect? No. He now remembered seeing them fall. Was he the only one alive?

"Bert…Rich." Nick coughed. "Larry. Guys, are you there? Can you hear me?" Witkowski's voice broke and he coughed again. No Answer. *Are they dead? Maybe dead—saw them fall.*

His ears picked up no sounds from them. He turned, straining his head a little more and saw dark lumps not far from him. Nick moaned. *What have I done? God, don't let me die. I must get that killer.*

The bastard that got them, lucked out. That's all it was, luck. No, it wasn't really luck. Witkowski knew they screwed up.

It seemed like an hour when Witkowski heard what sounded like a thousand sirens screaming to get closer to him. Through dim eyes he watched blue flashes of light bouncing off the buildings, from the bubble gum dome on top of the radio cars. His breath came in gasps but he still held on to his Smith & Wesson revolver, pointed in the direction the cold-blooded adversary had taken minutes ago, after the suspect fired his parting shot.

A minute later Witkowski heard the screeching of tires over the wailing of the sirens. A weak smile on his lips as a brother officer shouted, "Over here!" His buddy Joe Mantegna found him.

"Easy, Nick. Let me take that from you. You're going to be all right," Joe said as he pocketed Witkowski's .38 Special.

"The others. How're the others?" Nick whispered hoarsely.

Mantegna answered, "The rescue squad will be here soon."

Nick feebly dropped his hand on Joe's knee. "The others." Another cough.

Mantegna said, "We need to get you to a hospital."

"The others, Joe."

Mantegna turned his head toward the other men lying in blood. He knew they were gone. "I haven't checked them yet."

"I'll call Ruth when the ambulance takes you to the hospital." Joe looked into Nick's eyes. "You're going to be all right," he assured him again.

Witkowski closed his eyes. His throat felt dry. A tear rolled down the side of his face.

Sargent Paul Markov came over and said to Mantegna, "You stay with them. We'll check the area."

Seconds later one ambulance screeched to a halt. Two white clad people jumped out and ran over to the group of three bodies. Witkowski lay a few yards from the others.

"Over here! Get your asses over here," Mantegna yelled at the medical attendants. "Nick's still alive."

"Still alive? What does that mean, Joe? I'm dying? The others are dead?" He hacked. "I feel so weak."

"Don't talk, Nick."

Witkowski saw two blurry figures place an oxygen mask on his face and cut his clothes to find his wounds. The young woman appeared frightened and paler than he probably looked. The older man gently told her, "We'll get him stable and out of here quick. Get a tourniquet around his upper leg."

She nodded and went to work, slicing his pant leg with scissors.

"Where're you taking him?" Mantegna asked the ambulance driver as they put Nick on a stretcher.

"Church Home Hospital, it's the closest," the man replied.

Good. Not to the butcher place—City, Nick thought.

Baltimore City Hospitals, known all over the city and county as the facility you didn't go to if you wanted to live.

As the attendants carried Nick to the ambulance, he heard cops running all over the area, saw them point their guns at the empty windows of the buildings and at shadowed obstacles.

"Be careful youze guys. He still might be close by," Sargent Markov hollered.

"He's gone. The bastard's gone and I lost him," Witowski faltered in a low hoarse voice.

"Please sir, be quiet and lay still," the woman attendant admonished.

The driver of the ambulance left the scene at high speed and activated the siren. The movement of the ambulance jostled Witkowski making the pain intensify.

"They need to know." His voice weaker now.

She patted him on the good shoulder. "Okay. It's okay." Tears filled the woman's eyes as she tended to him. She shook her head.

Through the glaze distorting his eyes Witkowski noticed her tears. Her short dirty blond hair around her young face reminded him of a schoolgirl. Through the blare of the siren he heard her say to herself—he's lost so much blood. He watched as she worked over him and felt her gentleness. The type of femininity the killer put an end to twice. He prayed again, *God, don't let me die. Need to get him.*

Then blackness.

2

Witkowski woke in the hospital with tubes in his nose that burned. The two I.V. bottles dripped medicine and nourishment into his arms. Ruth Witkowski held his hand. He noticed her ashen and sour expression. Nick's hand squeezed Ruth's. The sides of her lips started to point up. She eked out a grin.

"How're you feeling, Nicholas?"

"Like hell," he answered hoarsely.

"At least you're feeling something." Her grin disappeared.

He frowned. "Whud the doc say?"

"You'll recover fully but it will take a while. It was touch and go but you still have your leg."

"That's a relief. How are you doing?"

"Oh, okay," she said in a tired tone. "I still have some money for groceries and gas."

"My medical will pay for this and I'll still get some kind of salary."

"You think we'll make it?" Ruth questioned.

Why did I marry her? "When I get well I'll be getting full pay again."

"And are you going to stay on the force after this?"

"Of course."

Just as Ruth opened her mouth to reply the doctor walked in.

"How are you feeling, Nick?" Doctor Markham asked while feeling Nick's pulse.

"Like hell."

"Same thing he told me," Ruth chimed in.

"He's lost a lot of blood." The doctor let go of his wrist. "Even with the transfusions you'll have to build your blood back up. Good news is no vital organs were hit and you'll have full use of your arm." Markham rubbed his chin, "You'll probably have a slight limp. Shouldn't interfere with your work. We'll have you out of here in a few days." He smiled, "You'll be able to run the streets again in two or three months."

"I feel better already."

Ruth turned her back on them and walked to a chair.

***

Witkowski left the hospital in a wheelchair, complaining to the nurse that he could walk.

"Hospital rules," Ruth admonished.

For the most part Ruth did help him to recuperate.

"Thanks for taking care of me, Ruth."

"Hey, I need you to get back on your feet so the big bucks will start coming in again." Ruth's smile seemed sincere.

Nick squinted at her.

She bent over and hugged him.

"Just kidding. I want you better. I don't like to see you hurt."

He hugged back and kissed her.

"You know, this is the best medicine I can have."

***

Three weeks later in the captain's office and still in some pain, Witkowski sat in front of Ed Kolodziejski's desk, questioning Witkowski about his part in the screw up.

"Before you write it in your report, I want to hear your take on what happened."

Witkowski had been interviewed in the hospital as soon as the doctor told the investigators it was okay. Now more of the same. Tired and still weak Witkowski said, "If I just would have…"

Kolodziejski put his hand up. "You were part of a team. The whole team screwed up. Remember that. Just tell me what happened since you are the only eye witness."

"You mean the only survivor and I don't feel proud of that."

"God has other plans for you. And your statement might help us get that mutt and get retribution for your fellow officers."

Witkowski told him the events that led up to the shoot-out. "We thought we had him, Captain. Then suddenly he came at us like a madman and shot us up." He stopped for a second, then continued: "In each hand semi-autos that never seemed to run out of ammo. We shouldn't have ran for the door. Thought he would run from us not attack us. I felt myself get hit but the others got it first." He paused and ran his hand over his salt and pepper crew cut. "Well, it was more like back and forth. I don't think he ever missed. Except maybe his last shot at me…it was close…but he missed."

Witkowski looked off and studied the photos of the captain's family on the wall. "Bert went down last, probably died then." He paused and wiped a tear from the corner of his eye. "I don't remember any details after he shot me the first time. I only remember getting hit and it stunned me. And I remember him running toward me when I was on the ground, firing and almost hitting me. He must have had some kind of weapons training, military or gun range."

The captain folded his hands on top of his desk. He cleared his throat. "Dr. Moreland will have some sessions with you to help you through the trauma. But I will say this, Nick. You've been on the force for only about a year. The others just had two years. We knew he was a bad actor. Lieutenant Briggs should have gone with you all or asked for a replacement." Kolodziejski looked over Nick's shoulder speaking low as if to himself, "He went on a bull shit call."

Witkowski leaned back and stared at his hands. "I shouldn't have let him get away."

"Nick, in a perfect world the department should have used the Tact team. Because of that sniper shooting two months ago it was supposed to be up and running. They finally got to the site but we might as well have had the Keystone Cops. They really need more training and leadership."

Kolodziejski didn't think Nick needed reminding that out of the sniper debacle, Baltimore formed the first Tact Squad and SWAT teams in the country. He would make sure that his men were not going to take the blame for this.

Kolodziejski studied the light fixture on the ceiling then dropped his head and promised, "Heads will roll on this but it won't be mine. When you get back you'll report to Lieutenant Janosko."

"It's not Briggs' fault. Blame me."

"Briggs is on administrative leave. Don't know when or if he'll be back. He's taken this pretty hard himself. But it looks to me like he'll be let go. I think he wants to go."

The chair squeaked when Kolodziejski leaned back. "You have appointments with Doctor Moreland, keep them. You are also on paid leave and getting rehab, so take the time and relax. Go see the tall ships."

Witkowski wasn't thinking of relaxing. He looked at the captain. "I have to get that murdering bastard, Captain."

"Relax, Nick. *We'll* get him—sooner or later," Kolodziejski assured.

They never had the chance. William Brocius felt the heat of the Baltimore police too close for him to engage in any more crimes in Maryland. He hid out for a few days in his old neighborhood along the Harford Road area. Plenty of friends to let him stay a day or two then he'd leave—his choice. Finally, nine days after the ambush, he fled the state and headed west.

***

Nick and Ruth Witkowski lived in the Highlandtown section of Baltimore City on Fleet Street, close to Patterson Park. Not far from where he confronted the killer. They had a row house with marble steps that Ruth scrubbed almost every week, just like her neighbors did.

"We've been married four years now and one year on the force with no promotion. All you've managed to do was get shot," Ruth complained after he came home from the meeting with the captain.

"Promotions take time."

He strode over to the sofa and dropped his weight on it. He placed his elbows on his knees and held his face.

"When are you going to get a decent job and one that pays more? Besides you're too short to be a cop."

"Look, we've been through this before. I've told you, I like being a cop and five foot eight is not too short. And dad retired from the police force with a pension and he's doing okay."

"I don't want okay. I want to have more," Ruth fumed. "Us to have more," as an afterthought. "I want to get out of Highlandtown. Move to the suburbs."

***

Oklahoma City, Oklahoma
1987

In June of 1987 the Witkowski's moved to Oklahoma City. Nick needed to get away from the liberal democrat policies that had a hold of Baltimore City. The mayors, of which the majority through the years were democrats, had made things more difficult for the police. Civilians were moving to the suburbs or out of state. When Witkowski left in eighty-seven the black population was around 59% and the white population, around 39%. The white population continued to decline. The black population stayed steady from 1970 to 2000. Overall, Baltimore's population kept dropping and crime kept rising.

Witkowski confided in his friend, Joe Mantegna, that he was looking elsewhere for police work. "I've had enough of the liberal politics here."

"I don't blame you, my friend," Joe said, and put his hand on Nick's shoulder.

Nick searched the *Police Gazette* and saw an advertisement that the Oklahoma City Police Department had openings for recruits and he applied. He had eleven years' experience and he left as a Sargent. The department accepted and Witkowski went through the Academy and started as a raw recruit—again.

***

"Nicholas, why'd you have to move me out here for more money?" Ruth nagged. "No wonder your parents named you Nickel Less, they knew you wouldn't make much." Ruth took a breath and spewed on, "And this god-forsaken desert you brought me to..." on and on she ranted.

Witkowski stopped listening to her long ago, but that was the last straw. The years of miserable existence together ended in nineteen-ninety-two with a divorce.

He was awarded the house in South Oklahoma City on Santa Fe Avenue. She got one thousand dollars and a plane ticket and flew back East. Nick said, "Good riddance, you money grubber."

After four years on the force as Sargent, Witkowski's goal was to become a detective, he had the talent for it. He left the Santa Fe Briefing Station on South Santa Fe Avenue and transferred over—in nineteen-ninety-three—to his new detective cubicle at the headquarters of the Oklahoma City Police Department downtown, known among the rank and file as Central. Shortly after, he was made detective investigator. In nineteen-ninety-six he advanced to detective inspector as a Master Sargent. Because of an opening, in nineteen-ninety-eight he was eligible to take the lieutenant's supervisor test, which he did and passed. Even with the increase in salary he kept his nice house on Santa Fe Avenue; it was almost paid for.

The Misanthrope

1964–1995

3

Oklahoma City, Oklahoma
1964-1995

"Daddy! That's daddy!" John hollered as he watched a taxicab go by. "No, honey, it isn't." Mabel, his mother said. She thought it sad that four-year-old John Cunningham saw every cab as his father's. Sadder still was the fact that he missed his father, Warren J. Cunningham. The man she gave her virginity to and married. The man she had loved. A year ago, she had found out the scumbag picked up fares and did the deed in the back of the taxi.

Most of the time Warren picked up prostitutes and that drained the family's finances. He would try to get as many freebies as he could. That didn't happen too often since he looked like a bear and smelled like three. Warren made the mistake of picking up one of Mabel's friends as a fare. She told the bear to go hibernate and promptly called Mabel and told her the details. It was an ugly scene when he came home. Warren also had the gall to brag about his other trysts during the fight.

"You bastard!"

Mabel grabbed a lamp off the table, yanked the cord and threw it. The whoosh of the lamp was drowned out by her scream of rage. Warren bounced it away with his arm.

"Bitch!"

He charged towards her with arms outstretched and eyes filled with rage. Mabel turned and ran. She fell over an ottoman and came down hard on her right arm. Warren grabbed her long auburn hair to pull her up.

"Ouch!" The pain was excruciating.

"You're worthless," Warren snarled and drew back his arm and punched her in the stomach. She went down like a rag doll. Warren J. Cunningham turned and stomped out. She was left alone with three-year-old John, who cried as he sat and watched the ugly altercation.

Warren never came back. She waited eleven months for him. Mabel was still lonely and in denial. Funds were running out and she needed to consider her needs and those of her son, John.

Mabel finally decided that she had to do something so she turned to the dark side for quick money. She headed for the *Blue Horse* bar. She still looked pretty, shapely, and sexy, so it didn't take her long to attract a man.

Mabel liked tall thin men with hair, but she didn't have much of a choice. She looked for someone who might be a financial provider. Also, age was not a problem if they looked like they had money.

The first guy's looks weren't bad or good. She thought he looked middle age and told him a hundred dollars for a good time. He didn't bat an eye, so she took him home with her. She was still naive and didn't realize the danger in taking a stranger to her house.

John, now condemned to live with his parent's mistakes, resided in a four-room bungalow with his mother in south Oklahoma City. With only one bedroom, John was forced to sleep on the couch when his mother had a man visiting to put bread on the table.

Four-year-old John needed his sleep and the uncomfortable couch felt like a rocky, wavy, landscape. He lay on the misshaped couch, his pillow over his head, trying not to hear his mother moan and the man grunt, "Yes, yes!" His mother's bed squeaking loudly and the man yelled, "Oh baby!" leaked through the pillow. Being in a small front room with the bedroom next to it, John heard every sound that emanated from within. He hated his mother.

Since most men found Mabel desirable, with her large breasts, it was not difficult getting men to willingly provide her with the necessary funds for John. She'd tell people, if they had the moxie to ask, it was because of Warren that she had to do this. He always cheated on her and slapped her. She thought she had no other skills, having dropped out of school at fourteen.

The fourth man she entertained, after eleven months of "mourning", moved in with them right away. Mabel thought having a man move in was steadier income. She had a parade of men move in, staying a couple of months, then they moved out. In between she had numerous one-night stands. She did whatever it took to keep John and her together.

Since the age of five, in 1966, John liked to look at the women's underwear section of the Sears catalog his mother always kept laying around. Sometimes when he heard his mother and a man having sex he would peek through the door and watch them with the catalog next to him. He hated watching them but he couldn't make himself leave. He learned women were to be abused.

Mabel would leave John with her sister, Doris. Then she went bar hopping with friends. She would drink, throw darts, and hang on men she didn't know— who paid the tab. She took them home with her or go to their place, or the car, it didn't matter. It helped when she smoked a joint. It relaxed her. She gave her body to get a man, so that he would help her keep John. She never confused sex for love. Every man she picked up was a paycheck. In four years, she had over thirty men but she was getting tired of the merry-go-round she found herself on.

"This is not good. I have to find someone who'll stay."

One fateful night at the *Red Dog Saloon*, Mabel met Harrold Wolf. He stood six feet, black hair combed straight back, chinless, small black eyes that were close together. His stomach cascaded over the top of his pants and lay there like a dead jellyfish. Somehow his legs never caught up with the rest of his body. Mabel told friends that he looked like a marshmallow on toothpicks, but she liked him anyway, blubber and all. When they did it—she never called it making love—Mabel complained that she got short changed. But she was true to him and he had a decent job as an auto mechanic. One day she would marry him and told her friends, "just wait and see."

Harry didn't think about marrying her. Why should he? He's getting the milk for free, why buy the cow? Too much responsibility to keep a cow. And he thought why ruin a friendship with marriage?

Standing at 5'3" she had to look up to Harry with her green eyes. Her long auburn hair fell three inches past her shoulders and styled in a spiral perm. Mabel was a good-looking, shapely twenty-three-year-old. Her hard-teenage years hadn't shown up yet.

John saw Harry come into his life at age seven. Two months after Harry moved in John caught the back end of Harry's hand for being in his way. Harry had been fired from his job because of his drinking. Now Mabel worked as a waitress supporting them. When she came home that day John tried to tell her what happened but she asked him *what he did to get the bruises.* John tried to stay out of Harry's way. He hated that fat fart who came into his mother's life. Would this be the last one? He resented what his mother had done to him and he hated her more.

John didn't know exactly when the followings started. He remembered that in the second grade, when he was eight, he liked to follow Lorrie, in Mrs. Myers first grade class. He felt superior to her. He knew that she was his girlfriend even though she had no idea. Mabel and her friends thought it was cute that John had a girlfriend. John would also peek into Lorrie's bedroom window whenever he found the chance. He loved her but noticed she just wanted to play with her dolls.

John continued to grow in immaturity. At puberty, he thought the world owed him. Or maybe it was life. He didn't really know; he just knew everyone owed him. The hell with their feelings and needs, he was the only one in the world that mattered. He was damned sure he would get his. Harry stood in his way. Through his teen years John tried to stay out of Harry's reach, but more often than he liked he caught the back of Harry's hand. The resentment built and would never go away.

"John, do your homework and pick up your room when you're done," Mabel told him.

Witch, he thought, as he looked at her and the boyfriend, Harry. "I'm seventeen and a man, but she treats me like a child," he muttered to himself. Easy for him, John did his homework quickly. *Mom should be proud of me.*

After he cleaned his room, John jumped into his 1961 Volkswagen Beetle, which he bought with money from doing odd jobs and stealing. He drove over to his former girlfriend's house and parked the Bug. He sat and waited until she came out of the house. Brenda had ended their dating when she met Charlie.

"There's the bitch now," he muttered.

Brenda left her house and started walking down the street. He started the car and followed her. She turned and walked up to her friend's house and John roared off. He circled the block, came around to Brenda's street again and parked in front of her friend's house. He got out of the car and knocked on the door. Her friend Gloria answered it.

"What do you want, John?"

"I want to talk to Brenda."

"Why?"

John pushed his way in. "Brenda, I want to know why you dumped me."

"Get out of here John. Gloria, call the cops."

"You bitch!"

Brenda felt the sting of his hand across her face before it hit. He had done that to her often.

"Get out!" Gloria screamed.

John shoved Brenda, gave Gloria the bird and left. She owed him. What did she owe him? She just owed him, that's all.

He got away with it. The police were never called.

***

At twenty Cunningham finally got a steady job. He drove a taxi cab, like his father. One night in nineteen eighty-two he picked up a highly intoxicated fare, on the corner of tenth street and MacArthur, just leaving a gentleman's club. She slurred an address he couldn't understand, so he drove her to Lake Stanley Draper, which was forty miles away. He found a dark secluded spot he knew about, parked then jumped in the backseat. She had been sleeping but woke up when he was on top, tearing her clothes off. She started to scream and Cunningham punched her once, almost knocking her out. She struggled a little and began making noise like a yell but not quite.

"Shut-up!" he said through gritted teeth.

Struggling to get in position on top of her, he covered her mouth with his left hand. Unknowingly he covered her nose also. The more she struggled the more he clamped down on her mouth and nose. She finally slowed her fighting, then she stopped. He kept on going. When he finished he removed his hand from her face.

"That was great."

He rose up and fixed himself. She didn't move or say anything. Her eyes were wide open.

"What's the matter, woman? You seen a ghost?"

She didn't move or talk. In the ambient light, Cunningham finally realized that she was dead.

"How the hell?"

She had died during the act with his hand over her mouth and nose. She suffocated.

Panicked, he jumped to the front seat and drove off. He headed east on Interstate 240, took an exit he knew that led to a few good secluded spots, picked one and dumped her in some brush. Then he covered her the best he could with the branches.

He left her there—someone's wife, daughter, mother, or sister. He didn't care. He felt elated. His first taste of killing. Even though it was accidental and unplanned, Cunningham loved the killing feeling. He was hooked and addicted.

There were two other victim fares he picked up, one in nineteen eighty-seven and one in nineteen ninety-five; both were in their twenties and single. After he dropped off each one, he came back in his car in the middle of the night, broke into their homes, raped them, then killed them and buried their bodies in Kansas.

Their relatives had called the police two and three days later and told them that they went missing. Waiting for the police both sets of relatives cleaned and straightened their daughter's apartments before the cops arrived—obliterating any evidence.

None of his victims were ever found and he was never charged.

4

Angie Tilghman, born in Phoenix in nineteen seventy-seven and reared in Oklahoma City, lived what most would call a normal life. That would be true until her parents were killed in an auto wreck on North MacArthur Boulevard, a week after her twenty-first birthday. She was hired by Cimarron Electric at eighteen, then left home. At twenty she bought a house in Yukon, OK. After her parent's death, her younger sister by two years, Cathy, moved in with her. They sold their parents' house and split the money. In January 1998, Cathy married Peter Mason and moved to Maryland with her husband, a stock broker with Legg, Mason Co. in Baltimore.

Men thought of Angie as a good looking twenty-three-year-old woman that some called beautiful, with stylish raven hair to her shoulders. Her skin was creamy smooth, without the slightest hint of wrinkles and no crow's feet. Her brown eyes always seemed to be smiling. Her straight and thin nose had the character of a Hungarian beauty. Her lips surrounded a sensual mouth that begged to be kissed. Angie's chin was angular and firm with no hint of being doubled. Her ears were delicate and her hands were smooth, she had a good body. Her legs were well formed, muscular and firm, giving her an overall sexy appearance. She had firm 34 size breasts and her rounded butt was the envy of women and men. All of Angie's beauty and sexiness stood on a five feet three-inch frame. The different thing about Angie was that she had a good personality to go along with her good looks. Sometimes this caused men to mistake her friendliness as flirtation. Angie tried to let a man know if he interested her by sweeping her hair behind an ear. With the others, she was just being friendly. But men being men, always had a tough time distinguishing the difference.

***

In December, nineteen-ninety-nine, Angie Tilghman first saw John Cunningham at a supermarket in Yukon Oklahoma a week after Thanksgiving. He caused butterflies in her stomach, so when she passed him, she gave him a flirty smile.

John smiled back. *Wow, is she flirting with me or what?*

The next isle over he saw her standing in front of some cereal. As he approached her, he could feel his excitement build. He sidled up to her.

"I like Coco Puffs myself.

"I think they are down the other end." Angie informed him. *Is that a dumb line or does he really like that junk?*

"Thanks. Say, are you doing anything for dinner tonight?"

"My, you are a bold one. What are you planning, Coco Puffs?" she said with a disarming chuckle.

John laughed long and hard.

"You are funny. I like that. I bet you have a good sense of humor too."

"I've been told that."

"Well, I think that is rare in a woman. I like that…very much."

"Thank you. I like a good sense of humor too."

She giggled and John chuckled.

"Does this mean you've accepted my invitation to take you out to dinner?" John asked.

"To a restaurant or your place?"

"To a nice restaurant, definitely."

"Well, I'll think about it."

John looked disappointed. He was not in control. Acting was a hard job for John Cunningham, but he did it when he had to.

"Okay," she said.

"Great!"

"Okay, I've thought about it."

"Oh?" John started to get tense.

"I'll take a rain check."

"Uh, okay."

"I have class tonight and I want to know you a little better."

"What better way than to have dinner together?"

"Can't tonight, but I'll see you in here again. Right?" She moved her hair behind her ear.

"You can count on it. When?"

"Tomorrow. Same time."

"I'll be here."

Angie walked away after she had committed herself to the mistake of seeing him again.

John Cunningham went home a happy man. Happier than he had been in a long time. He wanted her to be the diamond he had been looking for. Men would be envious that he had a woman like her, he thought. He would do everything in his power to make her his prize. His last girlfriend was no prize. He had misjudged her. Abusive mentally and verbally, she almost got the upper hand on him, but he managed to out abuse her and put her six feet under. She became his fourth victim since he started fifteen years ago. All four were still listed as missing persons, unsolved cases. He hid them wherever he could. So far, he hid them well.

FBI stats stated that serial killers had a minimum of three victims with a cooling off period. John was beginning to boil.

His job as a cab driver served him well, like his father. And like his father he raped and abused women. He hated women like most psychos. When he picked up a fare and liked what he saw, he would have them sit up front. Then he would take them to a secluded area where he would first threaten them with death if they didn't do as he wanted. Then he'd beat them and finally rape them.

Cunningham knew his luck would run out soon. He didn't care. He'd ride this train to the end.

He still visited his mother from time to time even though the sight of her made his stomach sick. It was more of a front. It might make him seem normal with people, he thought. Because of Harry Wolf, his stepfather, he never stayed long. He hated that man as much as he hated women, but never admitted it to himself.

Watching Angie

2000

5

Yukon, Oklahoma
Tuesday, May 30, 2000

John Cunningham closed his eyes and breathed deeply while his mind went into overdrive. He thought he could still smell Angie. That was more wishful thinking. Angie Tilghman had dumped him six months ago, and said he was too old, as old as his Volkswagen. True enough, he and his VW were the same age. Now he sat in his vintage 1961 Beryle Green, looked more like dirty gray, VW waiting for her to come out of the store. He was old enough to know what a fine woman looked like. So what, if he and his Bug were thirty-nine. He needed to see her, just watch her. Damn, he missed her.

Sitting in an old Bug with a dent in the hood above the handle and the windows down, wasn't being discreet. He didn't care, he wanted to get a glimpse of her. More if he could. Maybe even talk to her.

The wind blew through the car but it didn't cool his lust for her.

His heart raced when he spied Angie leaving the grocery store carrying two plastic sacks. John watched her head toward a white Mazda. Her short black skirt tight around her butt made her look even sexier. He licked his lips as he watched the wind whipping her ebony hair across her face. Dynamite sexy he always told her. The short time they were together it had been a challenge trying to persuade Angie to submit to him. She didn't. His increasing domineering behavior forced her to break off the relationship after two and a half weeks. Now six months later Angie walked to her car without him. Probably not even thinking about him—the bitch.

The urges to have, rape, and kill, came over him every three or four years which probably kept him off the radar. Psychotic killers usually have the urge to kill every few weeks or months. As time goes on the process usually speeds up. Cunningham had one of the longer time spans between murders.

Angie reached her car, put a sack down and unlocked the door. She turned and saw the Volkswagen. She froze for only a moment then jerked the door open, threw in the groceries and jumped in the Mazda. Locking the doors at the same time she started the car. Angie wasted no time in leaving the parking lot.

Cunningham watched as she sped away from him. He wiped the moisture off his upper lip. Chuckling to himself, he said aloud, "Why the hurry? I know where you live." He then laughed. Later he'd pop at her front door and surprise her. *Now's not the time.* He started the Bug, drove east on Reno Avenue and headed for home.

John turned into the entrance of the community where he lived off 10th street. He spat at the sign proclaiming, '*Pleasant Valley Mobile Home Estates*'.

"My ass," he snarled. "It's a shitten trailer park and there ain't no valley. It sure as hell ain't pleasant."

The trailer park had a mixture of wrecks, derelicts and a few somewhat nice dwellings that were still lightyears away from getting into the pages of *Architectural Digest*.

Cunningham followed a maze of what might loosely be called streets. He approached the back of the park where his old 12-foot-wide trailer nestled between two wrecks, one occupied. He snarled at his home, which was one step from being a wreck itself. He heard, then observed pieces of aluminum siding flapping in the wind. The outside, originally cream and beige, now muted to a dingy tan that rain couldn't wash away. The killer stubbed his foot on the broken cement path leading to his door. "Damn."

Cunningham at age thirty-nine, stood 5'10" and looked like Joe College. He had a lean athletic build. He carried himself well as he walked to the cabinet in the kitchen. He pulled a bottle of Jim Beam off the shelf. Carrying it to a battered, liquor stained sofa he plopped down and took a long swig, his green eyes tearing as the alcohol burned its way down his throat. He glanced at his watch: 5:11. He gazed out the window and brushed his hand over his rusty fly away hair.

"Looks like another liquid dinner," he said and took another gulp.

Angie arrived home and drove the car into the garage before the door ran all the way up. As soon as she stopped, she hit the button to close it. "Hurry, hurry," she coaxed the door. Shaking, she opened the door to the house and quickly checked the front and back doors. She had the locks changed after her breakup with that nut job, John. Next, she checked the windows. Satisfied, Angie peeked out the front window. No VW. She stayed at the window for ten minutes before she relaxed. Glancing at the wall clock she asked herself, "I wonder if it's too late to call Lieutenant Witkowski?"

She walked over to the table by an armchair that held the telephone. She picked up the receiver, pulled the aerial antenna up, then punched Central's numbers on the dial.

"Sorry, ma'am, Lieutenant Witkowski left for the day," said the answering officer.

"Would you give him a message saying Angie Tilghman will be in at 4:30 tomorrow to see him…if that's okay?"

"I'll leave him the message ma'am."

Angie called Mike Quinn next. Mike had been a close friend for two years but they were never intimate. She made it known to him that her feelings were platonic. She hoped she could trust him.

"Mike, can you come over? John is following me again."

"Is he at your house?"

"I don't think so. I've been checking since I got home fifteen minutes ago."

"I'm on my way, Ange. Oh, are you hungry?"

"Starving."

"Be there soon."

Mike arrived with a bag of submarine sandwiches. He kissed her on the cheek and laid the subs on the dining room table.

"Any sign of him yet?" he asked.

"No, and I've been looking."

"Probably not around then. I didn't see him or his Bug anywhere."

Angie walked over to Mike and hugged him. "Hold me."

The smell of her mixed in with light perfume made Mike forget about John and the food. "You're okay now, Ange."

She looked into his brown eyes and they seemed to radiate. She knew Mike loved her but she felt only friendship. Close friendship perhaps but not love. She "dated" him to have someone between boyfriends. Angie wondered how long she could hold him off before he wanted to make love. She disengaged herself from his embrace.

"Let's eat."

Disheartened, he said the only thing a guy could, "Okay." He took his OSU cap off and laid it on a chair.

"Oh, I forgot. I have groceries in the car. Would you get them for me and I'll set the table."

"I'm on my way."

He's so sweet. One day I'll send him on his way. Hopefully he will still be my friend.

6

Oklahoma City
Wednesday, May 31, 2000

Witkowski walked through two sets of automatic doors, at Central, waved to the officers behind the glass on his left and limped to the elevators. He passed through Homicide on the second floor and said good morning to three detectives who were at their desks. He opened the door to his closet size office and let it stay open. In front of his desk were two hard wooden chairs. On the right wall were framed pictures of him with the chief and mayor. He maneuvered left between his desk and a bookcase, squeezed around a four-drawer file cabinet and plopped into his high back leather chair. Witkowski rubbed his leg. His badge of courage, in the line of duty—to the men. Instead, his scars and bum leg reminded him of his failure to catch the killer, William Brocius. He twisted and placed his Stetson on a hook behind him.

His eyes floated down to a note. He picked it up. *Angie Tilghman wants to meet with you at 4:30.* Nick stared at the note, then put it in his pocket. *Still having stalker problems,* he thought. *Damn.*

"Good morning, Nick," Margaret Bollinger said sticking her head in the doorway. "Our morning pick-me-up is here."

Margaret had been Witkowski's secretary since he received his promotion to lieutenant.

"I hope you got the jelly filled ones," he ragged.

"Yes, and the crème, and the custard."

Witkowski twisted out of his chair smiling and followed Margaret to the coffee and doughnut table. Lieutenant Bruce Ritter stood there chewing a powdered jelly filled.

"Nick, my boy, these sure tastes great this morning," Ritter assured.

"Don't eat all the jellies," Witkowski emphasized as he grabbed a cup for his coffee.

"Rough morning, huh?" Ritter grinned.

"Not yet, but I'm sure it will get there."

"You boys grab your stuff," Margaret warned, "here comes the rest of the gang."

"Bruce, come in my office a minute," Nick said grabbing a jelly filled on the way.

When they settled, Witkowski asked, "How are your studies for captaincy coming along?"

Ritter sipped some coffee. "I'm doing fine, Nick. Studying hard. What's on your mind?"

"Remember the situation I caught with Angie Tilghman and that stalker who was bothering her?"

Ritter nodded.

"Well, it looks like he's back. I got a note this morning saying she wants to see me this afternoon. It's in your jurisdiction."

"If you're asking me if you can take that case, no problem. Go ahead."

"Thanks, Bruce. You sure you don't want it?"

Ritter grinned. "No. You're already familiar with it. Besides, that would be Art Morgan's case right now."

"Yeah. I'll talk to him, too."

Witkowski had a bad feeling about Tilghman's situation. He bit into his jelly filled and immediately felt better.

***

"He won't leave me alone." Angie cried.

She sat on one of the hard wood chairs in Witkowski's cramped office. Even with the door shut, her crying still penetrated into the Homicide room.

"I'm sorry but there is nothing I can do. He hasn't broken the law," Witkowski told her.

"Yes he has. He told me he was going to kill me if I didn't come back to him." Angie's voice was high pitched and strained. "When will you do something, when he kills me?" She sobbed uncontrollably into her Kleenex.

Witkowski leaned forward with his hands folded in front of him on the desk. He spoke softly.

"Angie, of the reported domestic violence incidents, less than one percent are slayings. Plus, you are one of the fifty-two percent of victims that call or contact the police in some way. Like you are doing now. Your chances are very good that this will be resolved in a satisfactory matter."

Witkowski hated this part of his job, the times of feeling helpless, knowing he couldn't do anything for the victims at that moment. He knew more than fifty percent of American female homicide victims are murdered by their current or ex-partners. He ran his thick hand over his crew cut. He hoped John would do something, but not harm her, so he, or one of the other detectives, could pull him off the street.

Witkowski unsnapped the cuffs of his blue Western shirt with brown horses' design and rolled up his sleeves exposing his beefy forearms. Before Angie came to the office he had asked Margaret to pull the file on domestic violence assault cases by the Oklahoma City Police Department. He found that nearly six thousand cases were reported. Most of them stemmed from women being pummeled by their husbands' or boyfriends' fists. He involuntarily shook his head and sat back.

Sucking in air through his nose and blowing it out of a mouth that could take a bite out of a quarter-pounder with ease. "I can give you some advice. Use an answering machine as well as caller I.D. He wants to hear your voice and aggravate you. Your voice, on a message from the machine might satisfy him wanting to hear you. Make it a long message." He looked down at his phone. "If he leaves a message, call me. Also, install a good home alarm system with a deafening exterior siren. And keep your doors and windows locked. If he comes around and threatens you again, call us." Witkowski handed her another Kleenex. "You can also obtain a VPO."

Angie looked at him through swollen brown eyes and between sniffles asked, "What's that?"

"It's a Victim Protection Order. Sometimes it works." He thought: *sometimes it can outrage a guy and provoke him to violence.*

"When we were dating, he sometimes got jealous but we're not dating anymore. Why is he doing this to me?"

"Some guys think they own a woman without marrying her. Not that a man owns a woman when he marries." Witkowski hoped he made himself clear. "I don't think it's a question of intelligence. It's of possession. You go home now and relax. Please call me if he tries to do anything you don't feel comfortable with. Here's my card. Use the cellular number. I have it on all the time and my area covers Oklahoma County and east Canadian County."

Witkowski leaned forward and handed her the card, then he steepled his fingers on the desk. "I might have a talk with him. Just to see where he's coming from. Don't worry, Angela."

"Thank you, Detective. It's Angie, Detective. Mom named me Angie cause she had a girlfriend named Angela. She said it would have confused her." She smiled at him.

"Oh. I'm sorry. Thanks for letting me know. And you can call me Nick."

Angie left police headquarters with apprehension. She never had a fear of someone stalking her. Especially one that she had dated. She was twenty-three and didn't need this happening in her life now. She was almost where she wanted to be in her life. This was her worst crisis since she left home at eighteen. If her mother were alive today she would know how to handle this. Angie didn't know and she didn't know what she should think—or do for that matter. Who could she turn to? Mike, her sort of boyfriend? She could use his help, before she dumped him—cruel, but necessary.

Looking over her shoulder, Angie opened the car door and stepped into her white Mazda. She sat for a moment and checked her eyes in the mirror. Still puffy. With the Kleenex, she wiped off some mascara that had streaked her face. She started the engine and rode off.

"I have to relax. When I get home, I'll soak in a hot tub of bubbles," Angie said aloud.

John saw her leave the police station. In all his thirty-nine years, she was the most beautiful woman he'd ever known. Her slightly teased raven hair that reached a little below her shoulders gave her a wild and exciting look that he loved. He wasn't about to let her go. John drove after her.

Almost to her house he had a change of heart and turned around. He decided to stop in Yukon for dinner. He hadn't eaten all day. Watching Angie made him forget about food but now it caught up. Too early to confront her. He'll wait until it's dark.

Watching through binoculars, Chad Payne saw Angie as she left police headquarters. He kept spying as John followed Angie.

"There they go," he muttered to himself. "That Angie is one hot babe."

Chad fired up his truck and drove south to I-40 and proceeded west. He exited the highway and went to Czech Hall Road and continued south. A mile later he turned onto his street. He pulled into his driveway, turned off the engine and sat thinking. *Two other guys sniffing after her. Some turd named Mike and idiot John. How to get rid of his competition? Mike shouldn't be a problem. John would be a messy problem.* Chad Payne came up with a solution. He would have to kill John.

***

Nine o'clock that evening John Cunningham couldn't believe his good fortune. He had sneaked into her backyard unnoticed and looked in her bathroom window. The sheer curtains were drawn. He watched her carefully step out of her clothes. He felt himself get excited. As she bent over the tub, he watched as she filled it with hot water, her full breasts swaying as she poured in the bubble bath. Angie walked toward the window to drop the blinds. John ducked quickly, cursing to himself at this turn of events. He headed back to his car.

"Shut up you damn dog," He muttered to himself as he reached his car and drove off into the deepening dusk.

"I wonder why Homer is barking," Angie said aloud. "He only barks at strangers or…" She froze in her thought. "Could that be John?"

Feeling sick in her stomach, she scolded herself, "Get a grip on yourself, Angie. You're getting paranoid."

She moved some bubbles around and asked herself, "What did Nick say when I told him I felt like I was getting paranoid? Oh yes, 'Paranoid is another word for heightened awareness.'"

She managed a slight smile at the thought and said, "Your awareness is heightened girl."

7

Oklahoma City shooting range
Thursday, June 1

Mike Quinn picked out two targets. Lance Pruitt also took two. They put on their ear protectors and strolled through the doors that led to the firing positions. Mike opened his range bag and retrieved a Browning Buckmaster .22 with a laser scope. Lance eyed the gun.

"Nice target gun."

"Want to shoot it?"

"No thanks. I know I can hit a long-range target with that. I need to practice my self-defense shooting."

Lance reached into his range bag, pulled out his Smith & Wesson Sigma .380 and loaded the magazine. He sent the target out to about seven yards, held the gun in both hands and fixed his eyes on the bullseye. Rapidly, he fired seven shots. He brought the target back. Six of the shots were in a four-inch group near the bullseye. The seventh shot hit a little high and to the right. Lance was satisfied with the results. Most self-defense confrontations occur within three to ten feet, so this guy would have been dead. Even at twice the distance.

Mike sent his target out thirty yards. He sighted the gun, red dot on the bullseye, and squeezed the trigger. Bullseye. Slowly squeezing off six more shots he hit the bullseye five times and one time in the nine ring.

"So, how's that for shooting?"

"Great. Are you doing this for fun or self-defense?"

"For both."

"You know the other guy is not going to stand there and let you shoot him from across the street. Unless you are going to be a sniper or do competition shooting, what you're doing is for fun. Not self-defense."

"Hmm," Mike said. He was thinking.

"For target shooting that's a great gun. For self-defense or conceal-carry it's not very good. Too long barreled and heavy. But, it's not useless. Any gun is better than no gun."

"What gun should I have?" He took off his OSU baseball cap and swatted at a bee.

Lance watched him, then he said, "The gun I have here is a three-eighty. This is the one I carry concealed. A .45 caliber is the best but it can get heavy and bulky. They do have some small .45s but they can kick hard. Especially for a woman."

Lance paused in his diatribe and pulled his magazine out. "They have some guns for sale here. After we're finished we'll look at some."

"Well, I don't know. I asked Angie out for dinner tonight but she said she would fix dinner for us. I should save my money in case she changes her mind. I don't have enough money on me. How much are they?"

"Don't worry, you don't have to get one today. We'll just look. Let's shoot."

***

Lance and Mike had been friends for four years. Mike had stopped in one of Lance's jewelry stores when Lance happened to be there. He bought a friendship ring for the girl he dated at the time. The girlfriend didn't last long but Lance's friendship did.

Mike worked as an X-ray technician for one of the hospitals in Oklahoma City. At five feet nine inches he stood an inch taller than Lance but was slightly thinner. The women found him likable and nice looking with his neat Fu Manchu mustache, although he was not an eyecatcher for them. His personality usually caught them.

Lance had the look that caught the attention of the ladies. Clean shaven he appeared much younger than his forty-two years. He was three years older than Mike but they looked about the same age. He worked hard at eating healthy foods. Lance hated winter and the cold and blamed it on being born in late January. An up-to-date dresser—had to be if one is in the jewelry business— his hazel eyes greeted everyone with a captivating smile. His brown hair had a pleasing style.

Lance lived by himself in the small Oklahoma town of Dry Creek, fifteen miles south-west of the capital city. He lived off the money he made with his three jewelry establishments. He didn't want to touch the money he inherited from his family's real estate fortune. Not being married saved money also. When the jewelry stores had a slow period, he left the stores in the hands of his managers so he could tend to his ten acres. He did all his mowing. He enjoyed some manual labor.

"I'm out of ammo," Lance said and put his gun in the bag. He studied his targets, grunted, rolled them up and tossed them in the trash can.

Mike looked over. "I thought you did well. You don't think so?"

"Yeah, I did fine. Now I'm ready for action." Lance chuckled.

Mike packed his pistol in his range bag. "I did good too. Look at all the bullseyes."

"You better be good with a gun like that." Lance watched Mike as he zipped his bag and asked, "So, you going over to Angie's tonight?"

"Yep."

"And you're sure she said she would make dinner?" he taunted.

"Yep."

"You're a lucky dog."

They reached their cars and before Lance hoisted himself into his pickup he said, "Have a good time tonight and tell Angie I said, hi."

"Will do." Mike hopped into his twelve-year-old 6000 SE four-door baby blue Pontiac.

"Time for me to settle down and find a good woman like Angie," Lance said to himself, "and maybe get married and have kids." He pointed the truck onto the main road.

8

Yukon, OK.

Later that day, Lance pulled into the Texaco on Garth Brooks Boulevard. He got out and opened the gas cap on his red '97 Ford F-150. While gassing up he saw John over on the next isle. John spied him at the same time. Lance nodded. John left his Bug and walked over.

"How's it going, Lance?"

"Okay."

Lance was wearing a T-Shirt under a short sleeve unbuttoned blue shirt. A slight gust of wind blew the shirt open, exposing his gun.

"Hey, you're packing heat."

"Sorry. The wind caught my shirt." *Damn it's against the law to expose your gun. Even worse, Cunningham saw it.*

"What kind is it?"

Lance was uncomfortable talking to John about his weapon.

"A Sigma three-eighty."

"What brand?" John asked.

Lance Pruitt didn't want to keep this conversation going but he thought maybe it would put some fear into John.

"It's a Smith & Wesson and a good concealable pistol. It holds seven rounds of ammo, double action and lightweight. A small or medium sized hand feels good around its' grip." He rested his hand on his shirt where the gun was. "I wanted a tough little gun and the Sigma fits the bill. I would bet my life on it." Lance smiled at Cunningham. Then he continued, "The other Sigma series, the 9 millimeters and enhanced 9, leaves something to be desired."

Smirking, John asked, "How come you're packing? Are you afraid of something?"

"Because I can. I have my cee cee license."

"I thought you might have it."

"And one never knows when something bad might happen. I feel better with it."

"Like what kind of bad might happen?" John Cunningham worried a little about running into Lance while watching Angie.

"You know a credit union got robbed again yesterday. The third time this year and it's only the first of June. I wonder if it's the sign on the door that invites crooks in."

"What do you mean?" Cunningham looked genuinely puzzled.

"Well, the sign says no firearms allowed, so those robbers were pretty sure nobody was armed in there. My bank doesn't have a sign and they haven't been robbed."

John responded slowly, now more worried. "I see what you mean."

Lance continued his spiel. "We have a God given right to self-defense. Besides, Mr. Colt or Mr. Ruger can be quicker than calling 911."

"Who's Mr. Ruger?

"You don't know."

"No."

"He's one of the best firearms manufacturers around. Ruger firearms are top notch."

The gas pump handle clicked. Lance put the hose back and jumped into his truck.

"See you later, John." He left quickly. He didn't like the guy.

"Yeah." Cunningham said to himself.

John thought he needed to be careful in Oklahoma. Some James Bond wanna-be might think following his woman would be a cause to protect her.

He pulled the gas hose away from his car and got in. He sat thinking he could deal with the police. It's the armed citizen he feared. They kill twice as many crooks as the cops do. On the other hand, they are five times more likely not to shoot an innocent person.

"I'm innocent," he said to no one. All he did was love Angie.

"Why did she give up on me?" He pounded the steering wheel then peeled out almost hitting a kid walking across the lot.

At ten o'clock that evening John decided to go to Angie's to make sure she knew how he felt about her. When he arrived, he saw a guy leaving her place.

John parked two houses down, still watching.

"That bastard just kissed her!"

As Mike drove off John raced out of his VW and up to her front door. He knocked on it and Angie opened it without looking to see who it was, "What did you forget Mike?"

John pushed through the door.

"Who the hell was that guy and what was he doing here?"

Angie screamed.

"Shut up you bitch and tell me!"

"I don't have to tell you anything. Get out!"

"Who is he? He can't be anything to you."

"You know John, I can see anybody I want to."

"Why him? You know I love you."

Angie sat down on the sofa with her arms folded. Homer came charging to the rescue, growling and barking.

"Shut up you damn dog!"

"John get out of here before I call the police," she said firmly. "Leave Homer alone."

Homer was still barking and growling ready to attack.

John plopped beside her. She sprang up and walked over to the phone and stood looking away from him. Sweat grew on his forehead. He could hear his heart pounding. His temper flared and he felt his face grow hot. She turned and looked at him.

"Bark! Bark! Bark!"

"John, you're an idiot if you think I'll ever be with you again. Just give it up. You lost. Go away and leave me alone."

John rose like a rocket. Homer followed, barking. He slapped her across the face. Angie fell back against a chair. He reached for her and missed. She jumped up and ran towards the kitchen. John grabbed her by the hair as she tried to get by him. Homer had his pant leg. He released her and kicked the dog with his other foot. Homer yelped and turned on Cunningham, this time his teeth sank into Cunningham's leg.

"Ow! You Damn dog!" He kicked him off and ran down the hall after Angie, with Homer at his heels barking and trying to grab his leg. Angie reached the bedroom and almost had the door shut as John forced his way in. He punched Angie in the jaw. She went down. He grabbed Homer from behind and threw him across the room. He then pulled Angie out of the bedroom, let go, and quickly shut the door as Homer came charging and barking. Immediately there was scratching and barking behind the door.

Groggy but full of fight Angie jumped up. "You leave Homer alone!" She raised her fists and he grabbed them and wrestled her to the floor. He pulled up her skirt and reached for her panties. In one violent motion he ripped them off. She continued fighting, hoping to escape. He slapped her face. His strength became too much for her to overcome. Angie felt him enter her with all the violence that raged inside him. She screamed and cried in pain. She thought she heard Homer barking. He sounded far away.

Finished with his criminal act, John beat her face twice. Blood flowed from her mouth and nose.

I have to stop him. She tried to scream again but couldn't. Weakly reaching for his hands to make him stop. She tasted her blood and knew she had to do something. He felt heavy on top of her, her head hurt. He punched her one last time and she almost lost consciousness.

Cunningham then wrapped his hands around her neck and began to squeeze. She choked and coughed. Her hands reached for his trying to save herself. Her eyes bugged, and near death she dropped her hands.

Homer continued to bark and scratch at the door.

Hearing the dog, he realized what he was doing; fear seized him. "Why did I do this?" He wasn't prepared to kill her, not yet. Where could he dispose the body? This went too fast. She wasn't a taxi-cab pick-up. He loved her. He hated her.

Confused, he jumped up and ran out of her house. He drove towards the perceived safety of his house, which was in Oklahoma City. John headed east on 10th Street and turned into the fourth and last trailer park on the left. He sprang out of his car and tripped up the steps. He found his keys, briefly fumbling, and finally unlocked the door. Once inside he locked the door and turned on the kitchen light, breathing hard.

A whiskey bottle sat on the second shelf in the cabinet. The ice clinked as he dropped it into the glass. Whiskey being poured over ice had a soothing sound. John needed to calm his nerves. He sat the glass down and turned on the kitchen sink spigot to wash the dried blood from his hands. He dried his hands carefully since they were sore and bruised. Then he carried his drink to an overstuffed chair in the living room and flopped down. Taking a long pull at the drink then gazing around the trailer he shouted, "What a piece of shit!" and threw the glass against the wall. He rose and went for the bottle.

9

Thirty-five minutes after Cunningham left Angie on the floor and ran, Mike Quinn drove onto her driveway and left his car. He knocked on her door. No answer. He tried the knob and it turned. He slowly entered and hollered, "Angie, it's me, Mike! Angie, I forgot my notebook. Why isn't the door locked?"

He walked slowly into the house. "Where are…"

He spotted Angie's limp figure on the hall floor, her clothes askew. Hurrying towards her, his heart pounding, he exclaimed, "My God, what happened to you?"

Gently lifting her up to a sitting position he examined her bloody face. He hugged her and said," Oh Angie, what happened?" Then he checked her breathing and found it shallow. At least she was breathing. She moved slightly. He went to get a sofa cushion, came back to her and gently laid her head on it. He rushed over to the phone and called 911.

After the call to 911 Mike heard a scratching sound at a bedroom door, then a bark. All the other doors were open. He went to the bedroom where he knew the bark came from and opened the door. Homer bounded out and went to Angie. He nuzzled her and whimpered.

Two uniformed officers responded to the emergency call and arrived right after the ambulance. The medics checked her over right away. Detective Art Morgan reached the scene seven minutes later. Nick Witkowski arrived ten minutes after Art. He had instructed dispatch to notify him of any calls involving Angie.

"Hey, Nick," the detective in charge of the crime scene greeted.

"What have you got, Art?"

"Not much yet. I did a quick interview with the man over there. He found her. Looks to me like someone beat the crap out of her, tried to strangle her, and raped her." Art Morgan shook his head.

"Let me know what else you find. She's a friend of mine."

"You got it."

Witkowski walked over to the para-medics who were just about to leave with Angie. She was groggy and pretty much out of it. They had put up a bag of liquid on a short pole attached to the gurney, to give her. Witkowski pulled aside the nearest one and asked in a low tone, "Can you tell me what happened?"

"Basically, three things, I think. Somebody beat the tar out of her and tried to choke her."

"Was she raped?"

He nodded his head. "I don't know if the beating and choking were before or after he raped her."

Witkowski face morphed into a scowl. "That son-of-a-bitch." He hated rapists and child molesters with a purple passion.

"We need to get her out now, officer."

"Just a sec." Witkowski bent over her to inspect the damage. Seconds later he nodded his head and the medics quickly wheeled her to the door and out. He felt himself heat up.

Art Morgan hollered to the para medics, "Tell them not to clean her up until I get there. I'll be behind you to finish the DNA."

"Okay, detective," one answered.

Witkowski stepped over to Mike. He was tapping his foot and his arms were folded across his chest. Mike watched as the paramedics wheeled her towards the ambulance. Homer sat next to him.

"You're Mike Quinn, right?"

"Yes, sir."

Witkowski also noticed the man looked pale and tense. The dog was looking at the man.

"Do you know why this happened or any idea who did this?" Witkowski led Mike away from the spot where Angie was raped.

At this point in time, Oklahoma City called their crime scene investigators, Technical Investigators. TI was busy gathering evidence, blood, hair, and samples of anything else in the vicinity that looked out of place.

"No. No I don't. But if I had to guess it was probably her ex-boyfriend, John. I can't believe this." Mike turned away as tears filled his eyes. Then went to a chair and sat. Homer jumped on his lap and he petted him.

"Why do you think that?" Witkowski could see Mike was upset and he had empathy for him.

"Because she's been having trouble with him following her."

"Do you know his last name?

"John Cunningham. The jerk. Find him…sir."

"Name's, Nick. We'll find him." Witkowski placed his hands on his hip and gun.

Mike put the dog down, stood and went to the door. They watched through the open door as the para-medics lifted her into the ambulance and took her to Southwest Regional Hospital.

"Did you notice any vehicle that might have been his?" Witkowski continued.

"No. But I know he drives a nineteen-sixty-one Volkswagen Bug."

"What color?"

"I don't remember. Oh, yeah. To me it looks like dirty gray or dirty greenish gray. Are you going to arrest him?"

"We'll question him first."

"Is that all?" Mike said annoyed.

"We'll canvas the neighborhood also and ask if anyone saw or heard anything. They're gathering DNA as we speak."

"Will that jerk give his willingly?"

"We can't force him now but there are ways. Whoever did it, looks like he probably left some." Witkowski inhaled and slowly blew it out. "We'll need your DNA also."

"I sure as hell didn't do it." Mike said angrily, stabbing his thumb into his chest.

"Just a formality since you were here when the ambulance arrived."

"I'm the one who called nine one one. If I had done it would I have stuck around. Would Homer come to me?"

"Probably not, but everyone is suspect. Relax, Mike, it's also used to rule you out as a suspect. It's just a quick swab in the mouth and it's done. We need to do this if it goes to trial. And, if this John clown did this, he committed a felony." Then Witkowski promised, "We'll get this guy."

Mike had been watching as the ambulance moved down the road and turned the corner. He turned his head towards Witkowski when Nick put his hand on his shoulder.

Witkowski lectured, "Mike, that guy is a molester, and a molester is a molester is a molester. He will not stop until we get him. He most likely has done this before to someone else. We will get him."

Mike looked down. "What he did to Angie…is…so wrong."

"Rape is to punish women. Nothing more, nothing less. Those types of men, and women criminals too, are exhibitionists. They want to be seen, show off. We will get the dirt bag," Witkowski reassured again.

Homer stood next to Mike and whimpered. He looked down.

"I'll come back for her dog and keep him. I know where her hidden key is."

Witkowski eyed him warily for a few seconds. "Okay, I'll let you do that, after we're finished here."

"Can I go to the hospital now? I want to be there for her."

"Sure. Stay in touch."

"Oh, I will." Mike bent over. "I feel sick to my stomach," Mike said and left holding his stomach.

Witkowski picked up the phone and called Central to put a BOLO on John's '61 Beetle. To be on the lookout for an old bug shouldn't be too hard to find. He'd have to get Cunningham's address from Angie when she's up to it.

"I'm going to the hospital and finish the DNA on Ms. Tilghman," Art Morgan told Witkowski on his way out carrying three evidence bags. "You'll have the paper work on your desk in the morning."

"Thanks, Art," Witkowski said.

***

Friday, June 2

After he left Angie at one in the morning and went back to her house to pick up Homer. They both slept together on his bed.

In the morning Mike's mind was clouded with grief and unbelief over Angie. After a night of on and off sleep, he phoned Lance. He thought Lance to be a sensible man and would know what to do. Plus, he was a friend of John's.

"That trailer trash is not my friend," Lance asserted.

"I know you talk to him, so I thought…"

"Big deal. He's a jerk, a loser."

"When I was at her house I overheard the medic say to his partner that Angie had been raped."

"What! That son-nuv-a-bitch. Why didn't you call me right away? Did the cops get him?"

"Sorry about not calling you but I was tired after I got her dog and took him home. And I don't know if the cops got him yet. Nick has an interest in the case."

"Good. Didn't John break up with her some time ago?"

"No, she said she broke it off but that he's been following her."

"You spoke to her?" Lance asked.

"Three days ago she told me. Said he still loves her."

"Yeah, if that's love his ass sucks lemonade."

"I want him stopped, Lance. The cops can't do anything until they catch him. Angie's been heavily drugged. So, she can't tell them anything now. He probably left his DNA on her. But getting the results won't be for a while. Makes me sick."

"Me too, buddy. I guarantee he left it. The shithead."

Mike sighed. "Her nose is broken and her right cheek bone has a hairline fracture. They might have to do reconstructive surgery."

Lance felt rage building inside of him. He hoped she wouldn't have to go through surgery.

"I also saw red marks on her neck like maybe he strangled her."

"The damn bastard. He'll probably go underground or run." Lance suggested. "Do you know where he lives?"

"No. Angie does, of course."

Thinking, Lance said, "Mike, you know the cops can't be everywhere. The citizens are supposed to defend themselves and the cop comes later to mop things up. I know he carries a Buck knife with him all the time."

"How do you know?"

"I've seen him pick his teeth, clean his finger nails with it. I think he would use it on her. He practically said so."

"What did he say?" Mike asked fearfully.

"I thought he was just blowing smoke at the time, but now I don't think so."

"What did he say!"

The harshness of Mike's voice gave Lance hope that Mike would be willing to help him carry out a plan that was formulating in his mind.

"He told me if he couldn't have her no one could. Then he stuck the knife into a tree."

"That sick bastard," snarled Mike. "Nick said he was an exhibitionist."

"I just thought of something. Three weeks ago, I read a book on Ted Bundy and he had a sixty-eight VW. The color looked like John's. Dent in the hood too. Sick bastard would stalk women, get them, then kill them. Dismember some of them too."

"Oh, crap. He's probably cut from the same cloth," Mike said.

"I have a plan. Meet me at Braum's in Yukon in half an hour."

"Which one?"

"Garth Brooks Boulevard."

"I'll be there."

They both arrived at the ice cream, hamburger, and small grocery store at the same time.

"How's that for timing." Mike said when he jumped out of his old Pontiac.

Going inside together they ordered two Braum's Burgers at the counter. Lance found a booth and sat. Mike sat on the opposite side.

Lance began, "That jerk has pissed me off royally. I want to tie his hands and feet between two cars and step on the gas."

"Damn, I wish we could do that." Mike wasn't smiling.

"Yeah, me too, but my plan is that we somehow bait John to come back to Angie's house, get him inside and tackle him. I'll put handcuffs on him then we call nine one one."

Mike rolled his eyes. "That idea sounds pretty lame."

"Lame? You got a better idea?"

"One eighty-seven!" came over the loudspeaker.

"That's me." Lance slid out.

"One eighty-eight!"

Mike followed Lance.

When they returned with their food and condiments Lance spoke. "Not much of a plan but he's not that smart. Plan is simple and so is he."

"I still think it's lame. On top of that it's no good. We can't set him up like that and expect him to fall for it."

"It'll work. Right after Angie gets home. We'll have her call him and say she wants him to come over and explain himself." Lance took a bite of his sandwich.

"Suppose he won't do it?"

Still chewing, Lance continued, "He will, I'll ask her to insult him. That kind of guy can't stand to be insulted by a woman. He'll come over in a flash. I know him."

"I can't do it. It puts Angie into too much danger. Come on man, you're smarter than that."

Lance had taken another big bite of sandwich and chewed nodding his head. He grabbed his glass of tea and took a swallow. "I know you're right. Dumb plan."

They laughed and agreed to protect Angie as often and as well as they could.

***

At four forty-six Witkowski makes a phone call to Lance Pruitt. "Are you busy?"

"Not at the moment. What's up?"

"You're sure you don't know Cunningham's address?"

"No. All I remember is that Angie told me he lives in a low-income trailer park."

"Do you know what he does for a living?"

"I know he drives a cab in the City." He used the word City as a shortcut for Oklahoma City.

"You know him well?"

"Not really. I get some strange vibes from him sometimes."

"Meaning?" Witkowski grabbed a pen and took his small notepad from his sport coat pocket.

"I don't know. To me he's weird sometimes."

"Like?" Nick thought it was a chore sometimes to pull info out of people. He was getting annoyed with Lance.

"Well, seems to me he has a mean streak. I think he's prone to extreme violence like killing someone or hurting them bad. And enjoying it."

"I guess you've seen that?"

"Yes. Once." Lance paused. "But what does a killer look like?"

Witkowski sat back in his chair. "Lance, they look like you, your friend Mike, your co-workers. They look like anyone and everyone. Ted Bundy was handsome, popular, polite, and well-spoken. David Berkowitz was a mild-mannered, soft, and pudgy killer. Only a few look like monsters, but monsters they are."

"Are you saying John is a serial killer?"

"No, but he could be…or not. We don't know yet."

"Gee."

"Just watch for him and let me know if you see him."

After they disconnected, Witkowski left his office for the day.

***

Sunday, June 4

The wind howled at forty miles per hour. Gray clouds raced across the sky as if they were trying out for the Indy 500. Shards of sunlight stabbed the ground at intervals. A good day to stay in bed, but Lance woke at seven to prepare himself for church. Going to church helped him keep a steady mind and to thank God for the blessings he received. With so much evil in the world, church was one place he found solace. Though he prayed every day, Lance needed the physical and social contact that church provided.

Before he prepared himself for the day, he knelt by his bed and looked up at the Crucifix. "Almighty God, Father, Son, Holy Ghost, thank you for keeping me safe during the night. Please give me the strength, wisdom, and patience to be kind and loving to people I come into contact today. Please protect my friends and relatives from all evils. Thank you."

Lance opened the door from the laundry room to the three-car garage and stepped down. He had his choice of the F-150, the Thunderbird, or the Corvette. Lance hopped into the Corvette and left.

After Mass was over Lance joined the parishioners filtering out of church. Herbert Brasington spied him, a friend from the parish.

"Yo, Lance. Howzzit goin'?"

"Hey, Herb. Okay. Just having a tough time forgiving an enemy."

"Father's sermon hit you hard about loving your enemies?"

Lance gave Herb a short version of Cunningham's crime against Angie.

"I just can't bring myself to forgive him, much less forgetting what he did. I can't pray for him. I know I should."

"I don't blame you, Lance. What will you do if you come across his path again?"

"I guess try to avoid him, unless he wants to start trouble, then I would probably shoot him."

"Gee, you better be careful. Maybe you shouldn't talk like that. At least in front of me."

"I can't confide in you?"

"You can, you can. I mean, let him start things first. I don't want to be a witness against you if you do something."

"He's my enemy now. I won't start anything but if he does…" Lance raised his head to heaven.

"Well, I hope you're prepared."

"Oh, I am."

One day, he was positive, he'd have to defend himself or a friend in a life and death struggle with John. That made him apprehensive. He had prepared for anything and kept himself in shape by exercising his body and his shooting skills. Praise the Lord and pass the ammunition. By God he would defend himself and others, if need be.

He knew John Cunningham was a strange bird and hoped he would go away. Except now that John had committed a felony against his friend, he'd have to help put the monster away. He expected John's fixation on Angie would be his undoing, by acting stupid again where he…or better, the police, could get him.

Witkowski's call to him Friday had unnerved him somewhat. Suppose Cunningham was a killer too, he thought. Could he handle him when push came to shove? He hoped so.

Lance then explained another thought to Herb, "There are some people in this world that shouldn't be here. And that jerk John definitely doesn't belong in this world."

Lance hated all the turmoil. He would rather concentrate on his jewelry business. Then again, maybe he didn't want the business. He thought about selling it to his competitor. Gary Smith had been bugging him to sell for the past two months. Lance was already a millionaire six times over. He could live very comfortably if he did sell.

Herb broke into his thoughts, "Let's make plans to go to Bricktown sometime soon."

"Great idea. I'll see what my schedule is."

They shook hands and parted. Lance promptly forgot the offer. His thoughts were now on Angie. He knew what he had to do.

The Heat Is On

10

June 5

Monday morning and still no paper work on his desk about Angie's rape, as promised by Morgan. Witkowski left his office and rode the elevator to the third floor. When the doors opened he turned and walked towards the Sex Crimes Unit's room. He said hi to the detectives as he past their desks and stopped at Art Morgan's. Art raised his head.

"What's, sup?"

"Have you tracked down Cunningham, yet."

"He's third on my list."

"So, no idea of his whereabouts?"

"Not yet, Nick," Art's voice tinged with agitation. "I *am* doing my job."

Nick raise his hands in surrender. "I have some time today to try to find him, is all. Remember I said that she's a friend and I can lighten your load a bit."

"Sorry, Nick. I had a bad weekend. What do yah need?"

"Have you had a chance to call the cab companies to see if he's at work?"

"No, I haven't. But if you want to, it would take a load off."

"No problem. I'll get right on it. Thanks." He turned to leave.

"Wait," Art said.

Witkowski turned back to Art.

"Thank *You*, Nick."

Witkowski smiled, gave him the thumbs up, and left.

Witkowski felt a tightening in his stomach. As a cabbie Cunningham had multiple opportunities to commit crimes or killings—and hide them. He reached for the phone book and found the listing for cab companies. He pulled his cell phone from his coat pocket and began calling. On the sixth call he got a hit.

"Yellow and Blue cab company. We have a cab ready for you now," a nasal sounding woman said.

"This is Lieutenant Witkowski with Oklahoma police department. Do you have a John Cunningham working for you?"

"Could you hold while I check?"

"Yes."

She came back two minutes later.

"Yes we do but he hasn't checked in for work since last Thursday. What's this about?"

"It's police business. Would you call me if he comes in?"

"Sure will, Officer. Give me your number."

"It's Lieutenant. Witkowski."

He spelled his name for her and gave her his direct line. He ended the call with a 'shit.' He ran his hand over his salt and pepper crew cut, which was beginning to have more salt in it than pepper.

Witkowski knew Cunningham was in the wind.

He picked up the receiver on his rotary phone and called St. Anthony hospital. He asked how Angie was doing.

"She's stable."

"Will I be able to speak with her?"

"No. Maybe in a week."

He hung up. A week. By that time Cunningham could be out of state—or country. He'd try to see her Thursday. That'll give her three days to heal and for him to work on two other ongoing cases.

11

June 6

Chad Payne had seen the TV reports about a rape in Yukon. The reporter gave a general area where it had occurred but not the name of the victim. Payne knew it was Angie who got raped. They said John Cunningham was the suspect and they were looking for him.

"I'm looking for him too. And when I find him, I'll kill him. Messing with my woman. I'm glad I was watching his ass too," he said aloud. "Now I wished I had followed him."

Payne had no idea where John lived so he asked his co-workers at the tech plant if they knew. They didn't. They knew John was or had been dating her.

Just before work ended for the day a worker heard that Payne wanted to know where Cunningham lived.

"Hey Curly Bill." The co-worker called Chad Payne by his nickname and wondered why he used that nickname. "I know John's address."

"Good. Spill it."

"It's forty-nine Glorious Lane in Oklahoma City. I remember, cause Angie said there was nothing glorious about the place."

"You sure it's number forty-nine?"

"Yup. Year I was born."

"What's the house look like?"

"It has to be a trailer. It's in a trailer park. That's what she said."

Payne thought for a moment. "Is it a nice place?"

"Heck, I don't know. Why?"

"Just wondering. Thanks." Payne walked away and left work before the shift ended.

***

Payne stopped at a gas station and bought a map of Oklahoma City and surrounding area. When he got to his truck he opened the map and spread it out the best he could.

"Shit, I need a magnifying glass to read this."

After ten minutes he found Glorious Lane on the map. He started the truck and drove west to North West Tenth Street. It took him fifteen minutes from the gas station to get there. He made a right at the sign that announced *'Pleasant Valley Mobile Home Estates.'*

"Damn. Even I wouldn't live here." He muttered.

It wasn't long before he found the place. Number forty-nine came up quicker than he expected,

He found a close spot to park. He got out and looked around. *Whadda dump.*

Payne walked up the metal steps and pounded on the door. He thumped on the door three times. He put his hands on his hips. Pounding on the door again he yelled, "Open up!" He tried the door knob—locked.

Payne attempted to peek through a dirty window next to the door. He couldn't see a thing.

"Yeah, you better be hiding you shithead."

He didn't know if Cunningham was home or not, and he couldn't break in—too many eyes. He decided to go home. Payne would have to figure out where he could be hiding—if he was. Payne was hungry and needed to eat.

He drove west on tenth then made a left onto Morgan Rd. and headed south. He got on I-40 at the interchange and followed it west to Yukon. Payne then took the Garth Brooks exit and drove north a few feet and made a left at the light into Braum's.

***

Cunningham had seen Payne through the slits in the Venetian blinds. He didn't know who that guy was but something about him seemed dangerous. He wasn't about to open the door.

More pounding on the door. Then he heard, "Open up!" Cunningham knew now—no way would he open the door to that Maniac.

John hit the deck when he saw the Maniac trying to look through the window. Good thing he had the door bolted also.

He then heard the Maniac call out, "Yeah, you better be hiding you shithead."

Cunningham's pucker factor went high. He didn't fear the cops as much as this guy. He knew a bad-ass when he confronted one. He decided to leave the Bug covered in the back and call a cab—as soon as the cretin left.

He went to the bedroom and grabbed a pillow case off a pillow and started to fill it with things he needed and wanted. He didn't plan on coming back.

12

June 8

Thursday, Witkowski went to see Angie in the hospital to ask about Cunningham's address. He hoped she could help. He had avoided the nurses to see her and snuck into her room. The sight of her shocked him slightly. There was a little bit of hemorrhaging still visible around both her eyes from when Cunningham had choked her. She also had swollen lips from the pounding she received. The bruises and bandages were upsetting to him. He'd have to get this mutt, but he really hoped someone else would. He would shoot the dirty dog on the spot.

He saw that she was awake and entered. She looked so helpless.

"Hi, Angie."

She mumbled something.

"I'm sorry. Are you still in pain?"

She nodded her head slightly. *Crap, he thought, she might not be able to tell me anything.*

"This won't take long. I have to ask this for the record. Who did this to you? Do you know?"

She nodded her head slightly.

"Can you write?"

She slowly nodded yes.

Witkowski took out his notebook from the inside pocket of his cowboy sport jacket. He handed it to her with a pen.

"Who did this?"

She wrote: john cuningham

Do you know John's address?"

She shook her head slightly.

"Do you know where he lives?"

She wrote: west o k c off 10th st in trailer park

"Do you know what it's called?"

She shook her head no. Then she wrote: its in the back

"Would that be north or west?"

Holding the pen and pad, she raised her hands in the I don't know position. She closed her eyes.

Witkowski touched her. "Are you okay?"

She wrote: yes tired

At that moment, the nurse walked in. "Time for your pain pill and antibiotic, my dear."

She stabbed a look at Witkowski. "Who might you be?"

"I am Lieutenant Witkowski, O'Casey Police. Police business. I had to ask her a few questions so I can get the man who did this to her."

"Oh. I'm sorry. Today she is not ready for visitors of any kind."

"I think my kind is very important…but I understand. She has been as helpful as she could."

He turned to Angie and retrieved his pen and pad. "I'll be back…" He lifted his eyebrows at the nurse.

"Give her three more days."

"I'll be back Sunday. Get well quick, Ange."

He got back to his car and grabbed his handheld radio. "Central, this is Henry 120."

"Go ahead 120."

"Is officer Phil Madsen in? If he is, patch me through."

"Hold on a minute."

Wish I'd remember his number. The one-minute wait seemed long.

"Phil Madsen," he said using his uniform mic.

"Phil, it's Nick."

"What's up?"

"Sign out a scout car and meet me at Reno and Council. I'll be in McDonald's parking lot."

"Okay."

They signed off.

Witkowski was leaning on the front fender of his car when Madsen pulled up. He walked over to Madsen's side and spoke through the open window.

"If I can find this John Cunningham we'll arrest him. If we don't get him today, I'll get an arrest warrant. Morgan's letting me do some of his work on Cunningham's case. I have to keep him informed."

"Okay. I'm ready."

"The victim gave me a general area where he lives. He's in a trailer park off 10th street. I checked the map and there are four separate trailer parks on tenth, side by side. My guess is that we should pick the worst looking one first. I remember the victim telling me it was a trashy looking park. Another thing she remembered was the sign. Pleasant Valley Mobile Home Estates. When she saw it, she almost laughed. Said she didn't."

"Those parks are over by Overholser Lake. There isn't a valley anywhere close for over a huner'd miles," Madsen said.

"What can I say?" Nick grinned.

"What's the vic's name?"

"Angie."

Sometimes Witkowski, and other detectives, used various names for victims—deceased, stiff, crispy critter, and the like, for dead or mutilated persons.

Angie wasn't dead so he used the term victim or vic. It kept him from having a too personal connection while investigating. It kept him sane and focused.

They drove separately, north on Council, made a left at the light onto 10th street heading west. They drove slowly, passing a rundown strip mall, saw a sign that announced *Pleasant Valley Mobile Home Estates*. They turned right onto County Line Road and Witkowski pulled into the first entrance. Then he pulled off to the side, stopped his car and dismounted.

County Line Road separates Oklahoma County from Canadian County.

"This has to be were Cunningham lives, it looks trashy all right. I'm glad this park is on the Oklahoma City side.

"She said it was in the back of the park, so we'll check the outside streets first. You take the first road on the left and I'll take the perimeter street. The only way we'll find it is if we spot the Bug."

"So, you don't know exactly where his trailer is?"

"No. Like I said, we look for an old Bug."

They slowly cruised along the streets. Half way through, at the far end of the park Witkowski stopped and slid out. He reached back into the car to get his cowboy hat and placed it on his head. Madsen just pulled up facing Witkowski's car. Madsen got out and walked towards him.

"Is this his place?" He asked.

"Don't know. But behind this beautiful domicile, is something covered with a tarp with tree branches on top."

"Leaves are looking freshly wilted," Madsen said.

"Right. They were placed there recently."

"It looks about the size of a Bug."

Witkowski turned to go up the steps. "Let's see if anyone's home."

Only room for one person on the landing so Madsen stood a step below ready to grab the door. Witkowski banged on the door like cops do when serving a warrant. He hated knocking on trailer doors because they swung out. Witkowski was actually by himself in this situation. He hoped Madsen would be quick if something happened. Nothing happened. No one came to the door.

Back at the cars Witkowski said, "My gut tells me this is the right place."

Witkowski lives by hard facts and evidence. He also pursues gut instinct and hunches, which usually win out.

"I could take a look under the tarp," Madsen offered.

"No. We don't have probable cause. If we did it without a warrant it could be inadmissible in court. If this place is not his it will get thrown out and the owner might get pissed and sue the department. Can't get a search warrant, again no P C, if this is not his place."

"I could sit on it."

"No. Could be a waste of time. I'll take the number and street and go ask the manager who lives here. We'll check with DPS and see if they can come up with an address, without a tag number."

The Department of Public Safety issues driver's licenses and has authority over the State Troopers. The OTC, Oklahoma Tax Commission, registers all vehicles, issues license plates and renews driver's licenses. Oklahoma does not have a Department of Motor Vehicles, DMV.

"Stay here Lieutenant. I want to mosey back here a bit. Check the front door again. See if it's unlocked, sir." Madsen walked back to the covered unknown.

Witkowski strolled back to the front door. They were on opposite sides of the trailer. Madsen looked down and stuck his foot under the tarp and lifted it a foot and a half. He couldn't see anything. Setting his foot on the ground he started to pad the tarp. Sides felt solid. With his knuckles he knocked on the top. It was solid metal. He ran his hands down to the left. Then he ran them over on the right. Felt like the shape of a Beetle auto.

He went back to the cars. He found Witkowski leaning against his with his arms folded.

"Well, what did you discover, Sherlock?"

"Felt like a Volkswagen. I think it's his."

"Okay. I want to confirm it. We'll talk to the manager, or whatever they call themselves, and match this address." He took off his hat and wiped his forehead with the back of his hand. "By the way, the front door was locked, so he's either out or inside watching us. Soon as we get the address to match the name, I'll type up an arrest warrant."

Madsen went around to his door and opened it.

"Oh, by the way Phil, thanks for giving me plausible deniability."

"What do you mean?" He smiled and jumped into his car.

The radio squawked on Nick's handheld radio. "Henry 120, come in."

"120, go ahead."

"Henry 120 we need a detective at 4779 Bossey Street, north west Oklahoma City, shooting victims. One deceased, one injured."

"On my way. Out." He hollered to Madsen. "Got a shooting call. We'll come back. Mount up."

Cunningham had seen them coming. He hurriedly closed the blinds but he could still look out. His forehead became moist as they approached the front door. He crept to the door and withdrew his Buck knife from his pocket and opened it. He stood in front of the door waiting. He flinched a bit as one of them knocked a hard knock as if he were serving a warrant. Cunningham was ready to get the first one at the door. He held the knife for a downward stroke to the neck and shoulder. When they walked away he peeked through the blinds and watched. He couldn't hear what they said. He knew it wasn't good for him. He rubbed the sweat from his forehead with his sleeve.

"Come on you pricks, let's get this over with." He thought about unlocking the door.

He had returned to the trailer to retrieve items he forgot when he bailed out after the visit from Payne. Bad timing.

He watched as they split up and the heavy gimpy one went for the front door again. Cunningham stood by it with the knife ready. He saw and heard the gimp try the knob. A bead of sweat ran down the side of his nose. He wiped it away. He was tempted again to unlock it but the thought of Angie popped into his head. Everything went silent. Fifteen seconds later he chanced to peek out the window. They were talking again. Then they must have got a call and they left. Cunningham breathed a sigh of relief. He put the knife on the counter and went for the bottle of whiskey.

"I gotta get outta here."

13

Friday, June 9

Witkowski glanced at his watch, almost eleven. He had been working on the Bossey Street shooting case since seven twenty in the morning. They were low lifes that had an altercation over a drug deal. He moved his paper work aside to a clear area on his desk. He sat back and ran his hand over his crew cut. He decided it was time for more coffee and just one pastry. He told himself that he would cut back one day. He rose and went to the snack table Margaret always kept supplied. He grabbed a crème filled this time and went to the coffee pot. He poured a new paper cup full. He looked around the room at the desks; only two detectives were at their desks and Margaret was at hers. Not wanting to bother them he limped back into his office. He had a computer on his desk that he hardly used but he would have to use it today. He was leery of it, afraid he'd blow it up, as he would say, and would sometimes freeze it or make it do strange things.

He took a bite of pastry and chased it with a sip of coffee. Then he booted up the computer. While it took its time to boot he thought about his talk with Angie yesterday. His mind dwelled on her situation now rather than on the two shooting victims.

He typed Cunningham's name into a secure Oklahoma State site and came up with his record. "Damn," he mumbled under his breath. Cunningham also had a juvenile jacket, which he couldn't get into. The open record revealed four arrests for carrying concealed weapons, every time a Buck knife. Three arrests for disorderly conduct and fighting. Five arrests for cruelty to animals. One for peeping. One for stalking and violating a VPO. He spent varying amounts of time in jail for all of them. Witkowski leaned back, took in some air, held it, ran his hand over his hair, then blew out the air.

He couldn't believe this was the only arrests in twenty-one years since his eighteenth birthday. He thought by this time there should have been a murder, or two. This led him to believe that John Cunningham was as slick as Clinton. His gut told him there was a skeleton in the closet, or underground, somewhere. He wondered what the juvie files held.

He called dispatch. "This is Witkowski. Where is Phil Madsen?"

"He's on patrol."

"Tell him to come to Central to my office. Please."

"Okay, L-T."

While he waited, he thought about Cunningham. He grabbed a donut and had another cup of coffee. When Madsen finally came in he was wired.

"What's up, boss?" The twenty-six-year-old drawled.

"Have a seat."

Standing next to the wall and filing cabinet, he pulled a chair by him and maneuvered his five feet eleven inches and one-hundred ninety pounds of muscled tanned frame into the chair. His brown military cut hair was uncovered and his hazel eyes had a gentleness to them that you won't find in most men. Born and reared in the small northern Oklahoma town of Harvey, it had left a mild-mannered personality, but when necessary, could explode into a concise fighting machine. The Police Academy honed his skills further.

"I know some day you want to be a detective."

Phil nodded.

"Well, I'd like you to help me with Cunningham."

"Sure. How?"

"By us brainstorming a bit. I checked his record and found some minor crimes that led to some jail time. He also has a juvie sheet that's verboten to us. My thoughts are that he has done something worse than what his record states. Like maybe a murder or two. Reading his sheet and what people tell me he's like, I can't see it any other way."

"Why's that?"

"There's something missing. If, I think it's a small if, he killed someone as a juvenile or as an adult but got away with it, then his record is leading us backwards."

"How's that?"

"He goes from murder to petty crimes. That's all he has. It doesn't fit with the profile. People like him always go from the small crimes and grow into big crimes, like murder, cannibalism, dismemberment, and so forth."

"Golly, Nick, you think?"

"I think he has killed people in his past. We have to consider him extremely dangerous."

"What makes people kill someone?" Phil wanted to know more.

Just then, Margaret walked in holding two paper cups of fresh hot coffee. "Here you go, gentlemen."

"You're a doll," Witkowski praised.

"Thanks, Margie," Madsen grinned as he accepted the cup.

"I'll take doll over Margie, buster."

Witkowski laughed and Madsen raised a hand in surrender, "Okay, okay."

She walked away smiling. "Let me know if you need anything else, boys."

Taking a sip from his cup Witkowski said, "What makes someone murder? There are three reasons for murder. Money, sex, revenge. I believe John Cunningham would fit two of the three; sex and revenge. And more emotion means more violence. The rape is another notch up. Sexual assaults are committed to punish women. Also, a serial killer is narcissistic. Everything he does, it's for his own satisfaction. He only cares about himself, and that's Cunningham. He wants her and nothing will stop him."

"Except us."

"Right."

"We gonna pick him up?"

"As soon as we know where he is."

"Maybe those cold cases where we haven't found the killer yet could be him."

"Could be. But we must get evidence then let the evidence tell us. Gut is good, but evidence is better."

"Shouldn't we get a search warrant?"

"It's being processed as we speak. He has been ID'd as the rapist."

"Has that address been confirmed?" Phil finished his coffee and chunked it into the trash can.

"Yes. We'll go in at four in the morn tonight. There'll be five of us."

"We couldn't do it ourselves?" Madsen winked at Nick.

"Right." Witkowski chuckled. "I'll let the others know and the Captain. Knock off early today and get rested up for tonight." He reached for his rotary phone.

14

Saturday, June 10; 4:00 A.M.

Witkowski and Morgan had decided not to use the Tact Team so the five raiders came in three vehicles; one unmarked and two black and whites. Coming in from two directions they blocked the street in front of Cunningham's trailer. Witkowski thought this was enough to put fear into Cunningham. He dismounted his unmarked. Nick had arrived from the east side. The other four jumped out of the two scout cars, including Art Morgan who drove one of the black and whites. Everyone wore a bulletproof vest. The three uniforms also had Kevlar helmets on. Witkowski wore his Stetson. No one spoke. Witkowski felt his back pocket to make sure the warrant was there. Then he pointed to one man, and pointed to the rear for him to cover the back door. He pointed to the three others and nodded.

Madsen took the lead as they ran to the door with their M-16s at the ready. Reaching the door, they covered the officer with a pry bar as he fit it into the seam of the door by the locks. Madsen hollered, "Go!" With a quick pull back of the bar there was a loud crack as the door splintered and ripped. He shoved the bar in deeper and pulled again. The door and frame gave way with enough noise that could wake the neighbors. With Madsen helping, the officer pulled the door all the way open. Madsen was the first one in followed by Morgan, then the bar officer, then

Witkowski. That was all planned at the briefing. Madsen yelled, "Police!" Lights were bouncing off the walls and furniture as they quickly "guessed" the way to the bedroom. The bedroom door was opened and Madsen yelled again, "Police! Don't move!"

They realized the bed and room were empty.

Witkowski ordered, "Check the other end!"

They charged out. Witkowski opened the back door for the man outside. He sped down the hall to help the others. Witkowski found the light switch and flicked it. The bed wasn't made and some drawers from a crappy looking bureau were hanging open—empty.

"Shit!"

The others came back. "The trailer's clear," Madsen said.

"Damn it. He's in the wind." Witkowski growled. "Check for the car."

The officer who had the back door went back out.

"Tear this place apart. Look for anything and everything." Witkowski ordered.

The officer came back in. "The Bug is here and so are the neighbors."

"Search the car."

He went back out.

Morgan went out the front door to confront the neighbors.

"Anyone here know the person who lives here?"

One person answered. "We don't know him, officer. He kept to hisself. Twernt no trouble though. Whud he'd do?"

"Anyone one here know anything about him?" He saw all their heads shaking in the negative. The crowd had grown to about fifty, with more coming. *They're like flies gathering on a carcass.* Morgan thought.

"What he'd do?" A woman shouted.

"We have a warrant for his arrest on a rape charge," Morgan said.

Gasps and some cries ensued.

A man yelled, "Good, we don't want that dirt bag here. But if we see him we'll protect our women." He turned to a man next to him. "Come on, Clem. Let's get our rifles."

"Whoa, there. You people call us, the Police, if he returns," Witkowski ordered.

"You bet we will," a woman shouted. "You can have him."

"All of you go home. Show's over," Witkowski said.

Madsen came up to him.

"We didn't find anything worthwhile. No notes. No indication where he might have gone."

"Any weapons?"

"No."

"Put the tape around the trailer and call a tow for the Bug."

Witkowski wondered where did he go? Where would he stay?

Madsen returned with a small phone book. "Bill found this. Looks like he was looking for a motel."

"Anything circled or underlined?"

"No."

"Alright. Wrap it up here and lock it up. Return to your regular duties," Morgan said.

Witkowski thought Cunningham didn't keep any trophies, or got rid of them or hid them. Bottom line, they never found any kind of trophies. An aberration.

Madsen went to tell the others. Witkowski got in his car and Morgan joined him. They went back to Central. As the lead detective Morgan would write up the report, and Witkowski started checking motels. The first one would be the Hampton Inn in Yukon.

15

Tuesday, June 13

Witkowski had done enough work this morning on the drug, murder case he caught last Thursday, so he closed the murder book and set it aside. There was no movement on that case. He, Madsen and other officers had knocked on the neighbor's doors. No one saw or heard anything. No one knew who their friends were, or relatives. The victims hadn't lived there long and now the whole neighborhood cringed in fear. They would make sure their doors were locked all the time now. One man said he hoped the killers would come back—he'd be ready with his eight-gauge shotgun. Witkowski had thought, another one, and told him to call the police first. At least not everyone cowered in fear.

Witkowski shook his head. People were not looking out for each other and they're not being vigilant.

Now he wanted to concentrate on finding Cunningham. He picked up the list of hotels and motels around the Oklahoma City area that Madsen had left. So far, together they had called three quarters of the list. He saw that the *Days Inn* on Meridian Avenue, just north of I-40, was next.

A few months ago, after making a few calls on the 1947, he decided to update his phone. It would be faster to push buttons than spin the wheel.

Headquarters was still hard wired—in case the power went out. He had maintenance re-install a hard-wired phone with push buttons. It sat next to his working 1947 rotary. It was part of his small antique telephone collection. He had two candlestick phones at his house as well as a 102 and a 202 by Western Electric. He also had another 'I Love Lucy' phone in addition to the 1947, officially called a 302.

He used his cell phone sparingly. He had only a limited number of minutes on it. He had decided that when they put up more cell towers and the price of the phones and services came down—he will opt for a better one.

"Days Inn. How may I help you?"

"This is Lieutenant Nick Witkowski with Oh-kay city police. Do you have a John Cunningham registered with you?"

"One moment while I check, Lieutenant."

While on hold he snapped his fingers to try to get Margaret's attention. That didn't work. He picked up his eraser and was about to throw it when the man came back.

"Lieutenant, I don't see a John Cunningham. So, he's not registered with us. I'm sorry."

"Do you remember a lean, well-built man with green eyes and rusty hair?"

"No sir, I don't. We get a lot of different people in here every day."

"He's around five feet ten inches."

"I'm sorry. That's not helping me."

"Yeah. Thanks anyway."

He probably changed his name and wore a cap. The calls were going to be useless, Witkowski told himself. But he'd keep trying. He rose from his desk, grabbed his ceramic mug and propelled himself to the coffee and donut table. He poured himself a cup. Looking at Margaret he said, "Don't you ever look up from your desk?"

She raised her head slightly and observed him over her glasses.

"Not when I hear fingers snapping. What did you need?"

"I have it now." He lifted his coffee cup and donut.

She looked down at her lap, then her left side, then over to her right.

"I'm not wearing a waitress uniform and I don't see any around."

Witkowski realized his mistake. "Well, uh, I was, uh, on the telephone and got hungry and thirsty. I thought I might get your attention and if you weren't too busy…"

"Nicholas, I declare, if that isn't the height of, of…whatever, I don't know. Just because I bring you donuts sometimes, don't always expect it."

"I'm sorry, Margaret, I wasn't thinking right. I was talking on the phone. You know men can't do two things at once."

"Ain't that the truth." She put her head down and went back to work. Witkowski turned and slinked back to his office. Margaret lifted her head and saw he looked penitential. She grinned.

"Next time throw an eraser at me."

He smiled and raised his cup to her. She had seen him. He then dialed the next number. When he finished the list, it was past lunch time. No hits. Again, he didn't expect any. He got up and walked to Margaret's desk.

"You want to go get some lunch? I'm treating."

"Sure, boss. Let's go." She grabbed her small cross over purse and put it around her. Witkowski knew she carried her gun in it. He approved.

After lunch Witkowski and Morgan decided to visit Cunningham's parents. Witkowski had said, if all else fails, go to the mother.

Morgan knocked on the door and Mabel Cunningham answered. They badged her and asked, "Can we come in to talk to you about your son?"

Mabel raised her hand to her mouth. "What's this about? Has he done something wrong?"

"That's why we want to come in, Mrs. Cunningham so we can ask a few questions," Morgan said.

Witkowski said, "You don't want us to do it on the porch with your neighbors watching. Do you?"

"No, no. Come in."

Harry Wolf sat in his chair as usual and said, "Who the hell are you guys?" He held a bottle of whiskey in his hands.

"Now Harry, these gentlemen are from the police department and they want to ask about John."

Before Wolf could say something Witkowski raced over to the lamp table next to Wolf and grabbed for the pistol on it.

"Hey!" Wolf yelled.

Witkowski had the gun in his hand. "What's this for?"

"I can have it. It's fer protection."

Witkowski checked it. Loaded. "You need a .44 Magnum for protection?"

"Damn straight I do. I have a crazy step-son. I can't stand him."

"Harry, don't talk about John like that," Mabel said.

"And that one," he pointed to Mabel, "Has the nerve to invite him over all the time."

"That's what we want to ask about," Art Morgan said, "Where's John now?"

Witkowski emptied the revolver, put it back on the table and kept the bullets.

"Whud you do that fer?" Wolf asked.

"For our protection," Witkowski answered.

Morgan asked again, "Do you know were John is?"

"Hell no and I don't give a shit. I hope he's dead somewheres."

"Harry!" Mabel had both hands to her mouth.

"Shut up, woman." He took a swig.

Witkowski led Mabel to the door while Morgan stayed and watched Wolf. He spoke to her softly, "Do you know where he is?"

She had tears in her eyes. "No. He hasn't been here for a while. What's happened?" She sniffled.

"He's wanted on a felony charge and we need to arrest him."

"Oh, no." She broke down and cried.

Witkowski walked her over to a couch and set her down. He took her hand and opened it. He gave her the bullets. She closed her hand and sobbed louder. Witkowski told her to keep the bullets someplace else.

Nick looked at Art and said, "Let's go."

Out in the car Witkowski said, "They don't know and she's distressed enough, poor woman."

"Yeah. Better get moving before he loads that gun and gives all of us a bigger problem."

Witkowski started the car and they left.

16

Thursday, June 15; 8:30 A.M.

The wind blew hard again, as it did half of the time in Oklahoma. The air had a chill despite it being mid-June. Overhead thick gray clouds were pregnant with water. The intense winds buffeted Lance's '57 Thunderbird as he made his way to see Angie. The hospital had released her Monday after eleven days. He parked his car in her driveway, got out and cursed the wind. *I need some rocks in my pockets to hold my butt down,* Pruitt thought. He knocked on her door. Angie opened it wearing a short loose gray skirt just above her knees with a light weight white sweater. She had on white ankle socks but no shoes.

"Angie, you're looking good," Lance complimented. Her bruised face had discolored to a shade of yellow while healing, and her nose had tape across it. She still wore a small white bandage on her right cheek.

"Yeah, right." She stepped aside.

"The bruises are healing nice."

"Get in and stop staring at them, they're ugly. My face looks like a disaster zone."

"At least you didn't have to have reconstructive surgery."

Lance followed her to the sofa. She sat and patted the spot next to her. He sat there. She looked into his eyes. He smiled at her. She didn't smile.

"I'm scared, John's bothering me again."

He stopped smiling. "He has a lot of balls. Looks like they haven't got him yet. He must have another place and hid his VW. Have you called the police?"

"No, I haven't called the police. If I did he would kill me."

"How would he know? How did he contact you?"

"Called my phone."

"I'm sure the police will be contacting you again soon."

"They have, a detective Art Morgan. I was afraid to answer."

"Ah geez, Angie. Call him now and answer his questions. I'm here. Nothing will happen to you. I know what happened. They already know what happened. I'm sure they want to know why it happened. I'm sure they want to know more about that idiot."

"Okay." Angie reluctantly called and answered the detective's questions.

After she hung up Lance said, "Hmm. I'd like you to get a cellular phone so you could call for help when you're away from your house."

"Oh, they are so expensive. And to get one that covers the city and half the state is more money."

"Well, get one. I'll pay for it."

"Thank you, Lance."

"I have a plan and it ought to work. Mike and I will wait in your house on a day you think John will show up. When he knocks, we'll answer the door and hold him for the police. Or, you call him to come over to your house and explain himself."

"Lance! That's just inviting trouble. I can't do that. I'm really afraid of him. I don't want him near me."

Lance wanted to get John himself. "Okay, okay. Make sure everything is locked and if he comes, call the cops."

"I can do that. And Homer might scare him away." She stopped for a few seconds. "Well, the last time Homer tried to help he did grab John's pant leg, until John threw him in the bedroom."

"Who's Homer?"

"My Heinz 57 dog. He's a mutt. He's out back. You want to meet him?"

"Uh, some other time, Ange. Mike told me he took care of your dog. How big is Homer?"

"He's medium built. He's black with white chest hair."

"I bet he loves you."

"Of course. I rescued him from a shelter. Now this is his forever home."

"You sure are cute. Call me if you hear from John…okay?" Lance made a move to leave. Angie grabbed his hand and leaned up to kiss his cheek. Pruitt couldn't tell if Angie blushed when she kissed him. He felt a tug at his heart and fought to ignore it.

"Uh, we'll try to protect you. Gotta go and get with Mike."

"That was a short visit."

"I told Mike I would call him," Lance looked at his watch, "right now. I'll see you later."

Lance Pruitt stood and so did she. She gave him a hug and he returned it.

Pruitt left her house with cold feet and slipped into his black T-Bird. He didn't know why he acted like that. Like a school boy. He picked up his cell phone and called Mike. Pruitt told him to meet him at *The Black-Eyed Pea* restaurant in south Oklahoma City, off I-240.

On the way over to the restaurant he thought to himself that Angie might be seeing someone else besides Mike. He thought the signs were there, her making excuses to Mike why she couldn't be with him, that it was okay for him to be busy with something else. Lance thought the trouble with Angie was that she acted very friendly and men liked that. She had personality plus. Men wanted a date as soon as they met her. Of course. She was also pretty and beautiful. She was pretty beautiful. Lance smiled. Though that wasn't a bad way to go. He had to be sure when the right woman came along. He wondered if she had ever really been in love with anyone. She picked the wrong guy with John.

Lance turned on the radio. Nothing good on. He clicked it off.

He continued his thoughts. Maybe she didn't want to see Mike anymore. If that was the case, he hoped that she would let him down easy. Well, there was no easy way to dump someone.

"If she wasn't going to see Mike anymore or if Mike stopped dating her, I could go for Angie myself." He said aloud. Then, he had a happy thought: *Suppose she's acting like that with Mike because she has her eye on me? And I ran because I didn't want a commitment now?*

"Lance, you are really dumb."

At the restaurant, Lance tweaked their plan to help Angie by nabbing John at her house. Then, to help Mike leave Angie he told Mike of his thoughts about Angie having someone else. Mike didn't like it.

"How do you know for sure?"

"I don't, but I can tell."

"Not good enough."

"Look, I could be wrong. Just forget it. Or keep it in the back of your mind. Do you trust her?"

"Yeah. I think."

"There's doubt. That's good. If she proves her trust or wants to continue dating, then it's okay."

"Would you trust her?"

"I'm not dating her, but if I were, I would look for signs."

"What kind of signs?"

"You'll know, Mike." Lance turned away. "Or, she might tell you straight up."

"Suppose she wants to be just friends?"

"Then be her friend."

The waitress arrived with the ticket and gave it to Lance. He paid her with a twenty, that covered a five-dollar tip, and they left.

Mike walked out with a feeling he wasn't sure about anything except he was pushing forty and wanted a family. He didn't want to have children at sixty. He'd miss their later years.

17

Friday, June 16; 10:00 P.M.

"I've got to talk to her," Cunningham muttered to himself while sitting in a chair at the Days Inn motel on Meridian Avenue. He'd been holed up in Oklahoma City for over a week and hadn't worked since the rape. He scanned the floor where his empty beer bottles laid scattered. He had stayed awake for twenty hours drinking and thinking about Angie. Cunningham hadn't eaten and he was hungry, tired, drunk and agitated. In his foul mood, he tried to formulate a plan to see her. A plan to talk to her, to tell her how much he loved her and wanted her. That he was sorry he hurt her. He would make her understand.

John whimpered. Suddenly he jumped up and screamed.

"Angie!"

Collapsing on the floor he sobbed.

"Why doesn't she see how much I love her? Why is she afraid of me?"

John stopped blubbering. He hit his fist against the floor.

"I'll kill her if she doesn't love me."

With his mind tired and his body in agony, John finally dozed off into a fitful sleep on the dirty carpet of the motel room. Emotions can take you to deep, dark places.

John woke with his head pounding. He squinted at the clock; 10:30 A.M. He staggered up from the floor, went to the bathroom and grabbed three ibuprofen tablets, gulped them down dry. He had to open a bottle of beer to wash it down. Then he picked up the receiver from the phone on the table and called for a cab. He grabbed his jacket, left the beer and headed out the door to wait for it. He had the cabbie take him to his mother's house.

"Hi, mom." His head felt a whole lot better. His hate for her had cooled down to a dislike.

"John, my baby," squealed Mabel.

"Hi, Harry," John said, hoping to keep the peace.

"You back again?" Harry snarled.

"I haven't been here in three months."

"It ain't long enough," Harry murmured. He picked up a bottle of Seagram's and took a swallow.

John squinted his eyes. "What did you say?"

Putting her hand on John's shoulder Mabel said, "You just don't mind him, John. For some reason, he gets grouchy when you come here."

"Tell the bum the cops were here looking for him." Harry took another swig of whisky.

"The cops were here?"

"Yes, John." Mabel said, wringing her hands nervously.

"What day?"

"Tuesday."

Harry looked at John. "You ought-ta be worried, ya bum."

"Shut your trap, old man." John clenched his fists.

Mable stepped between them. She was glad Harry was sitting.

"Are you hungry?" Once again stepping in as peacemaker.

"Starving, mom. Thanks."

"Now we have to feed the bum," Harry sneered and took another swig.

John glared at his mother's boyfriend, whom he hated more than anyone. He spotted the revolver on the table beside Harry.

"What's the hardware for? Harry, the wolf, gonna shoot someone?" he taunted.

"Yeah, you, if you don't shut the hell up and git yer ass outta here," Harry snarled. "No wonder the cops are lookin' fer you. Yer a pest and a bum."

John's blood started to boil. He reached in his pocket for the Buck knife, pulled it out and opened it.

"I should cut your gizzard out, lard-ass."

John walked towards him following the knife.

"Why you little…" Yesterday Harry had forced Mabel to give him the bullets and he picked up the re-loaded .44 and fired wildly. Missing, he shot again. John ran around the corner to the hall just as the Smith&Wesson roared a third time.

"Come back here you bum!"

"Harry, stop!" Mabel yelled while heading in the direction John went.

"You chicken shit!" John hollered from a bedroom. "You missed me, you hairy wolf." Even with the taunt, his heart was in his throat beating in high gear. He'd have to get out. The knife was no good now.

Two more times the .44 Magnum filled the living room with canon fire, the slugs going through the living room wall, across the hall, through the bedroom wall, finally imbedding in the far wall of the bedroom. John dove to the floor, unhurt. Harry staggered around the corner, past Mabel and towards the bedroom. Mabel followed him grabbing and pulling the belt on his pants.

"Stop, Harry!"

"There you are you bum!"

Harry pointed the .44 at John and jerked the trigger. *Click.*

"Damn, I only put in five." It wouldn't have mattered since he was swaying from the alcohol and Mabel yanking his belt.

John needed no further encouragement. Vaulting out of the bedroom he made a jab at Harry and missed him as he sped through the front door and down the street. Three houses down he slowed to a walk berating himself for running.

"I'll come back later and kill him."

He reached the end of the street, crossed over the highway and entered a drugstore. He found a phone booth and called for a cab. While waiting he walked into a liquor store next door. He bought two liters of *Jack Daniels*. When the cab arrived, he told him to take him to the car rental in Yukon.

Again, emotions can take you to deep dark places. John Cunningham was full of disturbing emotions now. The whole weekend, he took a chance and stayed in his trailer. He had parked the rental car two trailers down. Cunningham thought that since the cops were already here, he didn't expect them back.

He started to drink Friday night and stopped Sunday evening, falling asleep in the chair.

Before falling asleep he mumbled, *tomorrow I'll go see her.*

18

Monday, June 19; 1:00 P.M.

Lance and Mike were in Lance's truck heading toward Angie's house off Cemetery Road.

"Before we see Angie, let's stop at the slop shop and get something to eat," Lance announced. He guided his pick-up off Interstate 40 into the town of Yukon. As they entered Al's Place, Lance turned to Mike and said, "We can work out the details on my plan over a bowl of soup or whatever."

"That's why we're here," Mike said.

There were only two people in the place. That's why Lance chose it, not very popular but clean and Spartan. A few cheap tables and chairs and a picture of a buffalo were all the decorations. Lance picked a table in the far corner. He sat with his back to the wall. Mike sat opposite from him. The waitress was in no hurry to greet them and hand out menus. Finally, she sauntered over with chewing gum popping and she handed them menus.

"Afternoon boys. Whad-a-ya have to drink?"

"Water with a slice of lemon," Lance ordered.

"De-Caf."

"Be right back."

What a frumpy looking woman, thought Lance observing her large caboose.

"Quit looking at her butt and tell me what your idea is," Mike said.

"Angie needs to have John stop harassing her. I talked to her and told her we'd stay in her house from time to time until John comes over. When he drives up and starts pounding on the door we will appear and tell him to get lost. We'll let him know that we know what he's doing and we will stop him if we have to. We could even grab him then."

"Sounds like the same plan to me. It's simple and straight to the point."

Mike inspected Lance's face for a telltale sign that it was a joke. No expression appeared to confirm his assumption.

"You're serious. Like he's going to just roll over. Are you insinuating that we both be there all the time?"

"As often as we can both be there. We might have to restrain him and call the cops. Or…maybe leave things alone or have Angie live with me."

Mike shook his head.

Lance continued, "Another option is to have Angie invite him over, then grab him."

Mike shook his head again. "I think whenever we are with her and we see him pull up we call the cops then, don't wait."

"Sounds like a good idea. Maybe that's what we'll do."

They talked some more and finally figured it out again that any plan of theirs was a bad idea.

"I just want to grab his ass and bash his head into a brick wall," Lance snarled.

The waitress finally arrived with their drinks. They ordered their food.

"That was a delicious free meal," Mike said.

"I thought you were paying for it. You know I don't carry much cash on me."

"I thought you did, since you're rich."

"I won't be if I pay for everyone's meals." Lance thought himself as frugal, he knew Mike as being cheap. "Don't worry, I'll take the tab."

Smiling, Mike said, "Thanks, Lance." Then he added sheepishly, "I have only two dollars on me."

Lance ignored the comment, reflecting on something else. "Have you ever really been in love?" He asked.

Mike thought a moment before he answered.

"No, I don't think so. I'm probably a committed bachelor." He paused for a second. "Well, maybe kinda with Angie. Oh, I don't know. Why?"

"I have once. I was totally sprung. I still haven't gotten over her and it's been four years. You just don't know. When you think you have a perfect love and she leaves you, it's devastating. I think she was a player. Hell, I poured my heart out to her. I figured she got scared that a commitment was coming. She said I was smothering her and that I was too old. Damn, I was only fifteen years older than her."

"Fifteen years! That's a lot." Mike grinned.

"No it isn't. She had dated guys older than me so I knew that was crap. She was perfect for me. She was beautiful, had a sense of humor, neat, extremely neat, and her voice was music, so feminine. Making love to her was like nothing I've experienced before or since. It lasted about a month, a glorious, fantastic month. I *really* fell in love with her. Then one day she said it was over, just like that." He snapped his fingers. "Sometimes a taste of honey is worse than none at all."

"Speaking of honey, here comes Lulu," Mike groaned.

"How did she know we were here?"

"Maybe she followed us."

Lulu, who seemed to be poured into the skin-tight jeans she wore, swished toward their table.

"Hi, Lancie."

"Afternoon, Lulu."

"Hi, Mike."

"Yeah."

"I've got a message for you, Lancie, from your friend, John."

"He's not my friend, Lulu."

"You're so cute when you look that way." Lulu winked at Lance.

"What's the info, Lulu?" Lance asked in an exasperated tone.

"Oh, yes. He knows you and Mickie don't want him around Angie. She's a doll. I love her hair."

"Get on with it," Lance ordered.

"Well, he said, and these are his words, don't you two get in his way."

"What am I supposed to do with that info, turn tail and run?"

"Oh, Lancie, I love it when you talk dirty."

Lance ignored the rude suggestion and asked, "Why didn't he tell us himself?"

Lulu feigned a hurt look. "I don't know. Geez!"

"Thanks for the message. If you'll excuse us, Mike and I have to talk."

"Okay. I know when I'm not wanted. To-da-loo."

"Wait a minute. Where did you see John?" Lance asked.

"At *Betty's Boutique*…where I style hair for ladies and some bizarre guys. The ones who want to make a big splash. Oh, you should have…"

"I know where it is," Lance barked. "It's across the street from this place."

Mike got up and sneered, "Is he still there?" He headed for the window.

"No. He told me what to say, then he left."

"Of course, "Mike said as he came back to the table, "he knows your truck."

"I know. Okay, thanks, Lulu," Lance said.

"Bye-bye, boys."

Suddenly Lance commanded, "Stay away from John. He's totally bad news."

Lulu waved on her way out and spoke loudly, "He came to me."

Mike frowned as Lulu swished away. "That woman makes me sick."

"She likes all men."

"So. She won't get me. I wonder if she's always like that…weird."

"She can't help herself. That's the way she is."

"I'm surprised at you Lance. You're saying that's the way she was born? That she can't help herself?"

"I'm pretty sure, maybe."

"What about John? He can't help himself. He has to act nuts over Angie?"

"Well, maybe something happened in his past." Lance shrugged his shoulders.

"You know…your ass is bent. If that's the case, then child molesters can't help themselves, that's the way they were born. Or a person that does it with animals, they can't help it, that's the way they were born. And all the other sexual deviants out there. It's a choice, Lance, a moral choice. Or maybe more correctly an immoral choice. Someone doesn't just become goofy just because of their past. I know some men and women who had hard or difficult or weird lives as kids and they turned out fine."

Lance stared at Mike. Finally he said, "You might have something there, my friend. I've known some people who seemed fine for years, then one day, presto change-o, a different person, a different sex. Let's go."

As they walked to the truck Mike said, "I think it's odd John sent Lulu to deliver that message. She's such a flake."

"Yeah, she might be but damn John knew where we were." Lance scanned the area; no beetle bug. "Which means *he* probably followed us. We better get over to Angie's quick."

They were silent as they raced to her house. It took them seven minutes to get there; traffic and lights. She lived in Oklahoma City with a Yukon mailing address.

A half block away, Lance pulled the truck over and parked. He turned to Mike. "Let's go."

"Wait," Mike cautioned. "She's leaving her house. She's going to her car. Why'd she park outside?"

"Hey, that looks like John getting into that car," Mike announced.

"Where the hell was he hiding?" Lance exclaimed.

"He's following her. He's got a lot of gall." Mike had his face almost to the windshield. "We didn't need a plan. He's just given us one."

Lance started the truck. "We're following them."

"Be careful. Don't let him see us," Mike advised.

"I think he just sees her."

"Be careful anyway."

Lance moved the pickup slowly, making sure that he kept the other cars in sight.

They headed south into Mustang, taking Highway 152 east to 44th Street, hooking up with I-44, then splitting to I-240.

"Keep an eye on them while I'm driving."

They were two cars behind John who was one car behind Angie.

"She doesn't know John's following her. She doesn't recognize the car so she's not making a run for it," Lance said. "The good thing is the jerk doesn't know we're tailing him. The stalker is being stalked. Isn't that a hoot?" Lance grinned at the thought.

"I called her cell phone," Mike said. "It says no service for that number. She must have it off."

"Or there's no service for this area from that carrier. Either way that doesn't do her any good."

They continued driving east on I-240. They were coming out of the congestion.

"This is going to be tricky following them in mid-afternoon. I have to drop back. I think she's going to Draper Lake. She said she might go. She likes to take hikes."

"If she still doesn't know that John's behind her she won't be running and we can catch up."

"I hope you're right."

Shortly Lance took exit 11A and hung a right onto South Douglas Boulevard. Then took another right and drove west on North Stanley Draper Drive until Lance reached Midwest Boulevard and turned left. He was driving south now until the fork and went left on West Stanley Draper. Suddenly he slammed his brakes and made a hard left onto a dirt road. He drove on and spotted their cars 700 feet into the park and pulled up behind them. They jumped out.

"No one in the cars," Lance said.

"We'll follow that dirt path," Mike whispered.

"I bet the jerk managed to surprise her. I told her to be aware of her surroundings. She didn't listen," Lance fumed.

"Check for signs down the path," Mike advised, and led the way.

Lance followed a short distance then stopped. "Here. Footprints and a fresh broken branch leading into the woods. Looks like a struggle here." Lance explained.

Mike walked back and looked at the so-called tracks. "I don't see nothin'."

"It's obvious to me."

"Where'd you learn to track?"

"I didn't learn, it looks like fresh tracks."

"Do you have your gun?"

Of course. Do you?"

"Just my scared self."

"Great. No backup weapons." Lance shook his head.

Mike scanned the ground and found a large rock.

"This is better than nothing," he said looking at it.

Cunningham followed her along the path. She glanced back and began to run. "Shit." He gained on her quickly. Grabbed her and pulled her down. She managed to get away by stabbing her finger in his eye. He swore and ran after her. Caught her again and pushed her to the ground and jumped on her. Angie screamed.

Slowly Lance and Mike made their way along the path through the trees. A scream pierced the stillness. Running in the direction of the scream they came upon a small clearing and saw John sitting, straddling Angie. She was on her back holding his hands while he tried to slash her again with his knife. Her arm bled.

"Stop asshole!" Mike shouted. "Get off her!"

John jumped up startled. "You want her for yourself? You ain't gonna have her. Nobody will!"

"Don't be stupid, John." Mike said hefting the rock.

"Shut up twerp or I'll cut your heart out."

John's fierce eyes spied Lance.

"Well twerp, I see you brought the Lanceman with you. You think you're tough Lanceman?" John asked waving his knife; sweat running down his face.

"I might not be the toughest guy around but I'm as tough as you."

"We'll see about that."

"Put down the knife, John!" Lance ordered.

John didn't drop the knife. He lunged at Lance. Lance wasn't prepared for the sudden attack. The knife found its mark on Lance's arm as he held it up to ward off the blow. The force knocked Lance back and they both fell on the ground with John on top trying to slice him again. Mike dropped the rock and rushed over and tried to pull John off. John threw his arm back and stabbed Mike in the thigh. That was all Lance needed to push John off. He jumped up reaching for his .380. John charged again. His swing was wild and Lance jumped to the side catching the knife across his stomach, leaving a ten-inch gash but not deep. Lance now had his pistol out of its holster. John saw the gun, scowled and charged again. Lance fired.

John stopped and looked with disbelief at the red stain spreading on his chest.

"You've shot me."

He started for Lance again. Lance fired the Sigma again. John staggered back a foot then dropped. Mike went over to him and looked into eyes that saw nothing, pupils fixed wide open.

"Oh, no." Mike vomited, missing John's head by an inch.

Lance pushed his foot against Cunningham, he didn't move. Lance noticed his eyes starting to film over. He was dead.

Lance holstered the gun. Shaking from the adrenaline rush he walked over to Angie, who was still on the ground, crying. He picked her up and held her. Both of them shaking as she sobbed uncontrollably. Mike hobbled over, looking pale.

"You want me to call the cops?"

Yes…and an ambulance."

"Nice job, doc."

The doctor finished taping the gash on Lance's stomach. His arm had four stitches and a bandage.

"I've given you a tetanus shot and I'll give you a prescription of Amoxicillin for infection. In case the knife was dirty."

Lance took the prescription, folded it and put it in his pocket, where it would be forgotten and probably washed with the laundry. He would take a special formulation of propolis his personal doctor had made for him. Propolis was a probiotic made by honeybees to protect the hive from all kinds of microbes. Germs have no resistance to it. There are no super germs that propolis can't destroy. Lance learned this ten years ago and was happy that he did. It saved him more than once.

Mike Quinn limped around the corner using a cane. Lance looked at Mike's leg.

"How's the leg?"

"The doc said it will be fine. But I shouldn't do anything strenuous on it for a week. Eight stitches, a clamp, a patch and I'm good to go."

"They said we can maybe see Angie later this evening. She's traumatized so she's sedated. We'll do that after we finish with the police. Nick Witkowski wants us to be at the station after we're patched up and I feel like I'm patched. How about you?"

"Yep."

"Let's go then."

It was five o'clock when the guys walked out of emergency of Norman Regional Hospital and crossed the street to the parking lot. Lance drove his pick-up onto North Findlay Ave, made a right at North Flood Avenue, then hung a left onto West Tecumseh Rd.

"I wonder what they will do with us?" asked Mike.

"We'll be okay."

"I hope so." Mike wasn't that hopeful.

Shortly Lance took the ramp to I-35 North and headed towards Oklahoma City and Central Police Headquarters.

Witkowski eyed the two men sitting in his cramped office at Central. The clock read 7:00 P.M. They both looked tired and haggard. In their hands, each one held a can of Sprite. Mike let out a sigh. Lance took a sip of his soda. They jumped when the phone rang. It was his old Western Electric phone with that horrible ring one hears in the old movies. Witkowski liked that phone and old stuff.

"Yes…Okay…I'll tell them…Thank you, sir."

He gently replaced the receiver on the cradle.

"The DA said it was justifiable homicide. You won't be charged, like I told you. This is a formality. But they're still processing the crime scene."

He leaned back in his chair. "It sure didn't take long. What was it, an hour to review your case?"

"Tell him we really appreciated his putting it on the fast track," Lance said.

"He'd like that."

"I wasn't too worried. I knew we had to go through the steps," Lance said as he took another sip of his Sprite.

Witkowski smiled. "I say, chalk one up for the good guys. I'm glad the DA listened to me when I asked him to push it."

"Thanks, Nick." Lance took a bigger swig of soda.

"Yeah. Thanks, from me too, Nick." Mike raised his soda can to Witkowski.

"Well, you guys saved the Santa Fe Briefing Station and myself the trouble and paperwork of going after that guy and grinding him through the system. You also saved the taxpayers money by not having to take him to trial. I tell you Lance, I'm all for honest citizens carrying guns. As a matter of fact, I'd like to see open carry and Constitutional carry."

Nick sat forward and steepled his hands.

"Between you and me, I would have helped you smooth things out even if you didn't have a license to carry."

"I appreciate that, Nick."

"I wished youze guys called me or us first though."

"We weren't thinking. I was busy following and trying not to lose them," Lance explained.

"And I was trying to call her but her phone was dead or something," Mike said.

"We both didn't want to lose her," Lance said.

"Well, coming from Baltimore I can see how the armed citizen can help. But Balmer won't see that. The city is still in trouble and it's getting worse. The liberal democrats who've been running the city for decades are still sowing the seeds of poverty and disruption. The new millennium is not going to be good for Charm City."

Mike stood and leaned on his cane. "Balmer? Charm City?"

Smiling Nick said. "That's how the natives say Baltimore. The promo guys call it Charm City. I call it Harm City, when I'm feeling good."

"I guess we ought to go back to the hospital and visit Angie," Mike said.

"I hope she'll feel like visitors." Lance rose and threw his soda can in the trash. "Thanks again, Nick."

The men shook hands.

Lance drove his truck out of the police parking lot and headed back to the hospital. *What a long day.*

19

Tuesday, June 20

Lance Pruitt and Mike Quinn were trying to cope with the death of Cunningham. Both were still shaken that Lance had to take a life, albeit in self-defense. It was upsetting to them, especially for Mike so he decided to call Lance and talk about the shooting and Angie. The sun was well on its way to high noon when Quinn called Pruitt.

"Have you had breakfast yet?"

"Yes. If I didn't I'd keel over from starvation."

"We'll, do you feel like brunch?"

"I can eat again if that's what you mean."

"Meet me in Yukon at Al's Place in a half hour."

"Okay."

As Lance pulled his Ford truck into a parking place, he wondered what Mike had on his mind. He spotted Mike waiting at a table. He motioned Lance over.

"What's up, bud?"

"Let's order first."

After they got their food, from the same grumpy waitress, Mike took a bite, put down his sandwich and with a sad look in his eye he spoke.

"You know Lance, I've been thinking lately about women and how they act."

"So, you've come of age," Lance smiled.

Frowning Mike said, "I'm serious. I've been thinking that it is better for women to have as few men sexually as possible in their lives. In the short run and long. Men will pick that up or hear about how many love affairs they had. They will knowingly or subconsciously treat them bad. They will be in doubt as to her love for him. If she has sex with ten or thirty men, he will not believe that he is her true love. He'd be a fool if he did."

"Sir Henry Wotton, a wise man, once said, 'Love lodged in a woman's breast is but a guest.'" Lance bit into his sandwich.

"I do believe that," Mike said. "He was smart."

Mike took a drink of his soda. Lance started to say something else.

"Wait," Mike said. "I'm not finished. Most of us men have had less than three or four women sexually in their lives, unless they married early on, then it's less. My secret is I've had only two and one was a one-night stand. As you know having sex with women is great, right?"

"Yes, I'd say so. Even the worst one was great. I dare say your one-night stand with Penelope was great."

"Yeah. But there was no commitment. Conversely, if we fall in love with a woman, he *knows* this is it, she is the one. The woman on the other hand claims she's in love with each man she was with. Well, most of the time."

Mike drank some more soda. Lance waited. He didn't want to stop his friend's rant, even though he thought it was just a bit off base. Maybe even in left field.

Mike continued, "Okay, it takes two to tango, but it's always the woman's fault. If she doesn't open the door, he won't be able to come in." He looked down at his food and spoke quietly, "Except in a case of rape. But that's not doing the tango."

Lance thought for a moment about what Mike said.

"I think you're right about the tango. I've almost given up on finding someone. Usually if I don't pursue the issue it, or rather she, finds me."

He ignored what Lance said and continued, "Seeing Angie last night was rough. She had it rough. She never invited me in, so with her situation I'm going to tell her it's over."

"Did it ever begin with you two?"

"Maybe only in my mind. I think you're right though; she's seeing someone else. I guess we don't click…that way."

"I'm sorry, man. You do what you have to. If you can, and I think you can, still be friends with her. I know she'd like that," Lance remarked, smiling to himself. The issue for him now was he might ask Angie for a date when she gets better. There's no other person that he knew who was interested in her, except for himself. His road became clear.

"Remember this, my friend, another wise man, Benjamin Franklin, once said 'Keep your eyes wide open before marriage, half shut afterwards.'"

Mike eyed him quizzically. "I'm not talking about marriage. I haven't got to first base yet with anyone."

"Well, dating is a step towards marriage unless a person is a libertine."

"What the heck is a libertine?"

"A morally unrestrained person. Just out for a good time, not thinking about the consequences that come with an immoral life."

"Well, I know Angie is not the one I will be marrying."

"Someone will, someone will," Lance mused.

"I'm talking about myself. Let's finish eating and get out of here."

***

Witkowski heard a tapping on his office door jam. He looked up from reading the report on John Cunningham. "Yes, Margaret?"

"There are a couple of reporters here to interview you about the non-police involved shooting. The captain okayed it."

"He did?" Exasperated, he drew in air and blew it out. He didn't like reporters and always sent them to Larry Daye, the PIO. He felt himself getting irritated with the captain. "I'm not giving interviews."

"You might. One is Marissa Flint from the Daily Oklahoman and the other is Tessa Corbinelli from the Daily Planet."

"I know Marissa and she just wants to push her liberal agenda. The other, Contessa did you say?"

"Tessa Corbinelli, from the Daily..."

He waved his hand. "I know, I know, the Daily Planet. Are you sure it's not Lois Lane?"

Margaret rolled her eyes. "I'll tell them you're not giving interviews." She turned to leave.

"Wait. Send Marissa in. I'll see what she wants. The other one will have to wait." He didn't feel like putting up with the blowback that he would get from the captain for dissing the press.

Margaret returned in short order with Marissa in tow. Witkowski stood and pointed to a chair. "Have a seat, Marissa."

"Thanks, Nick, for seeing me. I won't take long. Just a few questions about the killing at Draper Lake."

Witkowski sat back and folded his arms. "Shoot."

"Oh, not me. I don't like guns. There should be more gun control."

Smiling without humor he said, "I agree. I always try to control my gun when I shoot. Just get on with it, Marissa. We know each other but don't take advantage."

"I won't take advantage of you," she smiled, "but are charges going to be pressed against," she looked down at her notes, "Lance Pruitt for gunning down an unarmed citizen?"

"Alright, you guys have got it wrong already." He moved forward, put his elbows on his desk and steepled his fingers. "The deceased had a knife and was using it on two men and a woman he had been stalking and watching for months. One of the men, Mr. Pruitt, was armed with a pistol, *legally*, and had to shoot Mr. Cunningham in self-defense. He had been attacked, with that knife, by Mr. Cunningham."

Marissa looked up from the notebook she was writing in. "I heard on the police scanners in my office that an armed man shot and killed a suspect. Nothing about a knife."

"Not all of the details go out on the scanner. You know that."

"That doesn't seem fair. It was only a knife."

"Now it's not fair, he only had a knife. Well, then he shouldn't have brought a knife to a gun fight."

"Are you serious?"

"Very, Marissa. He did the citizens of this state a favor by taking out the trash."

Witkowski leaned back.

"Can I quote you?"

"No. You'll probably get it wrong. Quote this. The thing is Mr. Pruitt broke no laws in this state. The DA is not going to prosecute. Mr. Cunningham was a wanted felon. The good guys got him."

"What was he a felon of?"

"Rape. We were looking for him but he went underground until yesterday when he surfaced from whatever sewer he crawled out of."

"I think Mr. Pruitt should be reprimanded for using deadly force."

Frowning he said, "Thank God it's not about what you think, it's the law."

She was about to say something else when he put his hand up.

"Interview's over, Ms. Flint. I have another one and I'm pressed for time." He stood and extended his hand. "Thanks for coming. Maybe you can get more info from Officer Larry Daye. You know him. Remember? He's in media relations."

Frustrated, she shook his hand and coldly said, "Thanks for your time, Lieutenant."

As she left, Witkowski grinned at her back.

Shortly Margaret came to Witkowski's office with Tessa Corbinelli. Witkowski was shocked by her perfect build and beautiful face. He remembered a cop friend in LA saying a woman that looked like her had a get-away face. Witkowski smiled and extended his hand.

"From the Daily Planet, right? Is Jimmy Olsen out there too?"

"Oh, no sir. I left him at the office," she joked.

Margaret rolled her eyes and walked away.

"Well, have a seat. Sorry about the hard chair but that's the only kind I have."

Still smiling, she sat. "I can take it. It can't be as hard as it is to get an interview with you. In fact, I was told by my editor to get a story about you."

"I apologize about the chair." Witkowski realized that he already said that and started to feel a little heated. He thought she was the most beautiful woman he's ever seen. A model's face. Yes, with a face like hers, she could get away with anything.

"So, you do work for a newspaper?"

"I have a confession to make. I'm not from the Daily Planet." She smiled and winked at him.

"You sure had me fooled. And being a detective, I should have caught that," he chuckled.

She laughed. She had a nice feminine laugh Witkowski thought. He started to feel dizzy now, then hot. *What the heck is wrong with me? She makes me sweat. No one like her would ever go for me.*

"I kinda work for a little neighborhood paper called *The Paseo*. I'm a journalism student at O.U. and a freelance writer. My editor, slash, boss, thought I might be able to get some ideas for stories from you. Like, you know, gangland shootings and things like that." She smiled.

"You're in the wrong state for that," he chortled.

"I also write sci-fi stories and hope to get a book published one day."

"I'm sure you will. I think you have talent." *And the looks.*

"How do you know?"

"Remember, I'm a detective and I detected it." Silly as that was, they both laughed.

Witkowski noticed that he already liked this woman. Her brown eyes sparkled merriment. He grabbed a pen and started tapping his desk with it. He noticed, and he stopped. She smiled.

"Ah, do you have any questions for me?"

"That's a loaded question."

They laughed again. Witkowski felt like he was in high school again.

Margaret appeared at the door. "Nick, a call from the hospital said that Angie Tilghman is well enough to be interviewed now."

"Thanks, Ms. Bollinger."

Margaret gave him a puzzled look, then left.

"I'm really sorry to cut this short but I need to get this woman's statement. We can do this again soon? Okay?"

"Sure, no problem, sir."

"Call me Nick."

"No problem…Nick."

Smiling, she stood. He stood. They clumsily shook hands, which he initiated.

"Uh, thanks… for coming," Witkowski stumbled.

"You're welcome," she said.

"And it was very nice to meet you."

"It was my pleasure to meet you, Nick."

Red faced and hot under the collar, Witkowski escorted her to the elevators then all the way to the front doors, which he opened for her and then slightly bowed.

"Thank you."

"No problem," he answered.

He watched her walk away. She had a nice wiggle.

"Hey, Nick, put your eyeballs back in your head." One of the officers behind the glass hollered. The other laughed.

Witkowski turned, walked to the elevator embarrassed, looked at them and said, "Ah, shut up."

That only made them laugh harder.

Death & Redemption

20

Wednesday, June 21; 6:30 A.M., MT

"I'm going to miss you. But I don't have to," Allen Gunnison remarked as Ronnie Tanner threw her leg over the Harley. Gunn didn't want her to leave. He wanted her to stay in Arizona.

Ronnie smiled at him as she flipped her blond streaked brown one-foot long braid over her right shoulder. She grabbed her helmet off the seat and placed it over the black do-rag coving the rest of her hair. Then she started her bike.

Ronnie didn't like biker men as potential lovers, only as friends. Seems like most of them were abusers or abused. She tried to stay away from that. Gunn almost had her convinced to be his woman or as he put it, his bitch.

"If you ever come to Oklahoma City look me up, Gunn."

With a wave and a roar, she sped off leaving Gunn watching her figure grow smaller by the second.

Thirty-two-year-old Ronnie Tanner left Phoenix because the company she worked for went belly up. She had been a secretary for a sand company. She gave most of her dress clothes to a friend. Ronnie could dress in any style and look good and be comfortable with all designs. Any style fit her shapely five feet and six-inch frame. The helmet with a face shield protected her hazel eyes from the wind and bugs. Her 36B cup breasts were nonexistent under her black leather jacket. She had a kind pretty face and sensuous lips, especially when she smiled. She goosed her bike to seventy-five. She loved the feeling of the open highway and the wonderful sensation of freedom. She turned on the radar detector and sped up to eighty-five. The 1340cc Heritage Soft Tail chewed the miles effortlessly. At this time of the morning I-40 was not busy.

She felt great travelling to her new job at Dolese Cement Company. "I can't stay away from sand," she laughed.

The bitch seat held two duffel bags tied across it. A small Arizona flag flew from the bitch bar. Two cars ahead of her were pacing each other at sixty-six miles an hour in a seventy mile per hour zone. She roared up on the one in the fast lane, flashed her lights.

"Get that damn cage out of the way, you moron."

They sped up and moved over as if they heard her. She flew by them with a surge of speed.

A few hours later she crossed into New Mexico and stopped at the welcome center. Ronnie grabbed a sandwich from one of the duffel bags and got a soda out of the machine. She went over to one of the picnic tables, sat and ate.

Thinking out loud she said, "It's going to be good seeing Angie again." She hadn't seen her in ten years, since Angie moved to Oklahoma City.

Finished with her lunch she hopped on her bike, started it, and roared off. She liked to travel by herself. She didn't think of it as being alone. After all she had Mr. Sam Colt with her—a Mustang 380 Plus II. She kept it tucked in her right jacket pocket for easy access, if need be.

Ronnie decided to stop at a Super 8 motel in Grants for the night. Dogged tired and a bed would sure feel good, she took the exit off I-40 and stopped at the office of the motel. Leaving her helmet on the seat Ronnie stretched as she strode to the office door. The tinkling bell didn't have any effect on the clerk. He didn't raise his head.

"Do you have any non-smoking vacancies?"

The balding man rose from his chair imitating a man of ninety. He shuffled to the computer, punched some keys and slowly eyed her.

"Double, queen, or king?"

"The cheapest."

"Double or queen are the same."

"Queen then, that's me."

She smiled. He didn't.

"How many?" His taco and onion breath sailed toward her.

Ronnie backed away. "Excuse me?"

"How many nights, how many people," he drawled.

"One and one."

"Room 145. Check out at eleven."

Ronnie took the key with a large plastic brown tag with 145 on it, drove the Harley around to the room and parked in front of the door. She grabbed the two duffel bags and unlocked the door. Tired, she dropped the bags, her helmet, turned on the air conditioner, removed her clothes and plopped onto the bed. It squeaked.

Ronnie woke at five, did her bathroom chores, took a cool shower and left. The day was already heating up.

After grabbing breakfast at *Burger King*, she headed east again on I-40. The flat top mesas were stretching on either side for miles. She would miss the beauty of the high desert. Oklahoma, she knew, had its own type of beauty. Angie told her she would be happy there.

Approaching Albuquerque, she spotted the city off to the right in the valley and Sandia mountain stood guard in front of her. She stopped at another *Burger King*, then a Texaco for her third fill-up. She guessed she had eight and a half hours more before she reached Oklahoma City, if she pushed it. The weather stayed hot, dry, and sunny.

Forty-five minutes later, Ronnie took the exit to Clines Corner. She loved the way people watched her pull up to a stop on her bike. *The women are jealous and the men want me.*

Swaying through the door, Ronnie went to the food counter. She looked around at the items for sale.

"What can I get for you?"

"They're sure proud of their souvenirs, aren't they?"

"Wouldn't know. You want something to eat?"

"Nah, just a glass of tea."

Ronnie looked again at the souvenirs. She noticed some things she wanted. The urge to buy something grew. The items were priced too high and she knew it. Besides, she didn't need it. More stuff to carry and she was supposed to be travelling light.

If I had gotten everything I wanted, I might be dead now. Not everything is good for me. But, when I get what I need, I realize that is what I wanted in the first place.

The waitress sat her tea in front of her.

"You seem to be in a good mood, honey."

"Oh, I was thinking, do I need any of this stuff?"

"Between you and me, honey, you can get this stuff cheaper in Santa Fe or Albuquerque."

Ten minutes later Ronnie mounted her bike, started it, and smiled at two young men walking towards the door. She roared off before they could react to her smile.

The Texas panhandle seemed more barren to her than New Mexico.

"Ronnie Tanner, this is your last meal before Oklahoma City," she told herself as she took an exit in Amarillo that led to yet another *Burger King*. She loved *Burger King*. No Big Mac's for her.

After her meal, she rode a few miles to *Flying J* to gas up. Browsing at the books on a table she found a copy of "Smokescreen" by Richard Gerhoff, took it to the cashier, paid for it and the gas. Then she headed for the rest rooms.

"Hey, baby-cakes, going my way?"

A greasy, longhaired fat man smiled at her.

"No. You don't have a full set of teeth."

Confused and speechless, the fat man watched her go into the women's room. When she came out of the restroom fat man was waiting.

"I don't like what you said."

"Why not? I didn't lie."

He grabbed her arm. Ronnie pulled into him and brought her knee up fast. Two seconds later he grabbed his crotch, air rushing through gaps in his teeth. She walked to the exit door of the store, turned around and saw him vomiting. She smiled. *The employees aren't going to be happy with him. And so close to the men's room.*

Ronnie noticed that the change in scenery from Texas to Oklahoma was almost as abrupt as the state lines. There were more trees for one thing. She liked trees but not too many. Oklahoma was also a little greener. The green was a new experience for her.

The Harley ran effortlessly. As the sun lowered itself behind her for the night, she felt the coolness. Invigorated, she rode on into the twilight.

Weatherford seemed a good place for a pit stop. Pulling into a gas station she filled her tank then walked to the restroom. The stars shown through the station's lights. The air smelled of hay, or was it wheat? The way to live was fresh air smelling of grains.

When she reached Yukon, Ronnie took the Garth Brooks Boulevard exit 136. She pulled into the Hampton Inn to spend the night. She dismounted her bike and stiffly walked toward the office. By the time she settled into her room she was too tired to call Angie. She washed her hands and face and removed her clothes, leaving only her panties on. Ronnie pulled down the bedsheet and slipped under. Too tired to turn out the lights she went to sleep instantly.

21

Friday, June 23; 8:30 A.M.

Lance Pruitt owned three *Glitter Jewelry Company* establishments in Oklahoma City. He hired three competent and loyal managers to run the stores while he travelled the country buying jewelry bargains. His upbringing made him an honest and caring jeweler who wouldn't sell junk. He had medium to high quality products and kept his prices as low as he could. He didn't believe in gouging the uneducated public with overpriced gemstones, gold and silver that others would markup 300% to 500%.

He also bought and sold numismatic coins as well as gold and silver bullion coins to discriminating customers. He called his computer, Quark, for today's gold price opening. Quark answered, "It opened at nine A.M. New York Exchange. That was one half hour ago at two hundred and eighty-five dollars and thirty cents per troy ounce."

"Thanks, Quark."

"Is that all?"

"Yes. Shut down."

Lance parked his truck in the lot next to his store on North Pennsylvania Avenue. As he slid out, he spied an unmarked police car. He stopped. He waited until Witkowski reached him.

"What's the occasion?"

"Sorry to barge in on you at work but I'd like to wrap things up with Angie's situation."

Lance didn't know what that meant but he said, "Sure. You've come to the right place. I've got Quark."

"Quark?"

"My computer. Extremely advanced. Y2K never affected it, he fixed himself. I'll show you."

As they walked slowly to his store Nick asked, "What do you mean 'he fixed himself'?"

"You know last year and the first week of this year how everyone was worried the computers were going to crash because of a date glitch?"

"Yeah."

"Well it saw the problem and corrected it—on himself, by himself."

"Oh, wonderful."

Lance let the remark go.

He and Nick entered the store on north Pennsylvania Avenue, greeted the employees and went to his office. Each store had a private office for him and the managers to share. This particular office had a large Spanish desk, made in Santa Fe, which Pruitt had shipped in. On the floor in front of the desk lay a Navajo rug. Western and Indian art by Frederick Remington and William George, hung on the walls. A six-foot cactus stood in one corner. His computer, what Lance called an atomic QC, completed the décor.

The computer was a little larger than a regular home desktop computer. It had a flat screen twenty-three-inch stand-alone monitor and a larger than normal Central Processing Unit, the brains. Two, nine-and-a-half-inches high, Altec Lansing external speakers stood close by. The best thing about the computer seemed to be that it was twenty years ahead of anything else, civilian or military.

Before Witkowski could comment on the fancy office, Lance said the command "ON" then introduced Witkowski to Quark.

Quark said, "Welcome Lieutenant."

Nick whispered to Lance, "It knows my rank."

"Sure. He knows everything. I just talked to him on my car phone."

Lance began explaining the workings of the QC. "Instead of computer chips or integrated circuits, this Quantum computer uses atoms. It's a billion times faster than a Pentium III PC or a personal computer. The atoms are natural tiny calculators, having a natural spin or orientation—the spin can be up or down."

Lance was animated, using his hands to explain. Witkowski stared at the computer. The large flat screen impressed him.

Continuing Lance said, "With digital technology, everything is represented by 0s and 1s. The atom's spin pointing up can be 1; down can be 0."

As Lance droned on Nick just nodded. He was half-listening. That flat screen still fascinated him. He could use a computer like that. No, he'd have to have someone else run it.

Got it?" Lance asked.

Witkowski just looked at him. Lance started again. Witkowski tuned him out and thought about how to get better at using a computer. *Why bother? I can get other people to do it.*

"That's basically how it operates."

Nick blinked at him. "Yeah?"

Pruitt could tell that Witkowski's eyes had glazed over. He laughed at him. "I see you're underwhelmed."

"To say the least. But I do like the flat screen."

"In a few years you'll be seeing them everywhere."

Lance Pruitt felt that he needed a powerful computer like this. He seemed to always want the latest and greatest gadgets.

At the turn of the new century in January, Pruitt was one of a handful of wealthy people in the world with a Quantum Computer. He felt this was the beginning of the artificial intelligence era. No one could use this computer but Lance. The computer would not allow it. It used face, voice, and touch recognition.

"No keyboard on this?" Witkowski asked.

'Watch this," Pruitt said. He sat behind his desk and waved the machine on. Then he typed in details on the heliograph keyboard that lit up on his desk, details of John, Angie, Mike and anyone else he could think of. He decided he would have dossiers on his friends and enemies since it seemed to him that he was always helping his friends out of trouble. It would also find murderers, kidnappers, and all other crooks faster and more accurately.

When he finished typing, he spoke to the computer.

"Quark, I have typed in some information, we want to know what is going on with Angie Tilghman."

Within seconds Quark said, "Angie has someone else watching her. He is more dangerous than the deceased John Cunningham."

"What is his name?"

"Chad Payne. He has another name. His real name."

"What is it?"

"I don't know it. I am working on it. He has a sealed Maryland juvenile record."

Nick looked at Lance. Lance shrugged his shoulders.

"Why does Angie draw these kinds of men to her?"

"Because she's beautiful and friendly which draws attention from men. Attention she has received from her birth. They instinctively love her and want her or be with her."

"Seems, you don't really need a keyboard," Witkowski said.

"Not really. Most times it's faster talking to Quark."

Lance looked at Nick and asked, "Do you have any questions for Quark?"

"Yes I do." He then asked his questions about Payne and about a couple of other cases. He wrote the information on his notepad. When he finished, he put it back inside his jacket pocket and thanked Lance…and Quark.

"I could've had Quark print out a hard copy."

"That would have been good, but I like the old fashion way. I need to check this Payne guy out."

Lance wanted to tell him something before he left. "Yesterday I found some interesting stats that Quark came up with."

"What was that?"

"I was asking about the murder stats in Oklahoma City compared to Baltimore, for nineteen seventy-six. Quark said Oklahoma City had forty-six that year."

"Yeah. What am I going to do with that?"

"You told me before that the three officers with you on that night call were killed."

"Yes, and that's a bad memory for me. Thanks for bringing it up."

"I don't mean it like that. I was just comparing. Baltimore had two hundred homicides that year. Man, that's a scary city."

"It's a larger city, Lance, and more compact. Not spread all over creation like oh kay cee."

Lance thought for a second then acquiesced, "Point taken." He didn't want to battle with Nick.

"Still, I believe the murder rate will go up. I'd say more than double." Nick said.

"Really? You think it will?"

Witkowski nodded and appeared a little sad. He wanted to change the subject. There was another reason for his visit.

"I'd like to stop by your store again when I have more time and pick up a surprise for Tessa."

"Who's Tessa?" Lance grinned.

"She's a special lady I met Tuesday at the office."

"Dang, you're moving fast."

"Gotta strike while the iron's hot." Now Nick grinned.

"Let me know when. We'll make her happy."

After Witkowski left, Pruitt checked his business interests, investments and personal finances. It took longer to read the info than to pull it up. When he finished, Lance told Quark good-bye, and used the command: off. That shut down Quark. He could have waved his hand. It only worked with Pruitt's hand—no password needed.

***

At 12:35 Lance left the store and hopped into his truck. He drove to Hideaway Pizza restaurant on Northwest Expressway where he wouldn't be disturbed to ponder the details from Quark about Angie.

While eating his pizza his cell phone rang. He flipped it open.

"Hello."

"Lance, you know my friend is coming from Arizona to help me and I'm sure she needs a job. Would you consider hiring her?"

"Sure, give me her number."

"She's staying at the Hampton Inn in Yukon."

"Room number?"

"Don't know yet. She hasn't called."

Lance had to think about that a second. "Okay, let me know when you know. How are you doing?"

"Fine. No problems yet."

"Good. I'll talk to you later. Bye."

22

Friday, June 23; 10 A.M.

Chad Payne almost slammed the door off its hinges as he rushed out of his small rent house observing the day. The sun shone brightly as it usually did in the southwest. No clouds were visible in the blue sky and the temperature, a comfortable 78 degrees. Payne thought, *this is great weather and hardly any wind.* He decided to take the day off from his job.

At age forty-six Payne had no woman now, but had five ex-wives. With gray, brown, curly hair, slightly over his ears, women found him attractive in a dangerous way. He usually kept a two-day beard on his face. His facial features favored the actor David Tennant. His six-foot height contributed to an aggressive split personality. He was strong but thinly built; this disarmed people to their detriment. He tended to run hot and cold and had cold blue eyes which always seemed to be wide open. His sharp nose bent to the right from having been broken in a bar fight. From his thin lips came smooth talking—his ally. Born in Baltimore he had to leave Maryland, at age twenty-two, on short notice. He arrived in Oklahoma City in 1997 by bus, his usual long-distance mode of transportation. He didn't stay long in any one city, typically just five years then he'd head out; he had to. He left dead bodies in Baltimore, Cincinnati, Louisville, St. Louis, and Kansas City that were never solved. He felt Oklahoma City would be no different. As far as he knew he left no finger prints or any DNA. The authorities in Maryland had his finger prints but they were sealed in his juvenile records—under a different name.

His beat-up twenty-five-year-old Chevy pickup waited for him in the driveway. He hopped into his truck, the tires spinning a little as he drove off to Angie's house. For two miles he listened to a Led Zeppelin CD playing until he came to Angie's house. Thinking she was at work, he didn't know about her being hospitalized and now released, he checked her mailbox which stood next to the street. A street side mailbox that made it easy for him to go through her mail.

Today there was a postcard from her sister Cathy with a return address. He wrote down the address. Angie had told him once that she had a sister.

He had found out from co-workers that Lance had killed John, which pleased him to no end. Saved him the trouble. Now Payne thought he had clear sailing in his ongoing quest for Angie.

The truck crawled onto the driveway. The door creaked as he stepped out. Then, he walked over to the gate that led into the backyard and went through. A six feet high wood stockade fence surrounded her small backyard. She probably thought it was more secure. Her neighbors also had that type of fence. Payne liked it because no one could see him. Homer, the dog, was not on patrol…good. The grass felt soft through his shoes as he made his way over to the bedroom window.

"Well, I'll be damned. She planted some cactus right under the window."

He glanced around and found a shovel leaning against the wall. Picking it up he dug the cacti out and flung them over the fence to a neighbor's backyard. After he finished, he went to the gate and fixed it so that she couldn't lock it. Satisfied with his work he walked back to his truck and left.

Chad Payne had dated Angie two years before John came on the scene. He still proclaimed his love for her. With John out of the way he would try to get her back. Mike would not be a problem. Payne knew some martial arts and he had his weapons. His uncle Terrence had instructed Payne when he was sixteen and seventeen on how to use firearms in a combat situation. His uncle knew Payne had a record and nicknamed him, Curly Bill.

Terrence, known to everyone as Mister B., also owned a sporting goods store on Eastern Avenue in Essex, Maryland, a suburb of Baltimore. Payne's lengthy juvenile record, that was still sealed and under a different name, did not stop him from getting weapons. Mr. B. gave up helping Payne since he always ran afoul of the law on minor charges, driving without a license, petty theft, and one for stalking. At age eighteen he changed his name to Chad Payne and had some minor adult records with that name. One for shoplifting at a Baltimore suburb, Dundalk, Maryland's S.S.Kresge five and dime store, and two for assault and battery. No one knew about the chain of bodies and dead cops in Baltimore. Or, for that matter, the multitude of other crimes he committed in other cities. In nineteen seventy-six he went on the lam, left Baltimore and finally ended up in Oklahoma City. For the most part, the law didn't know about the killings, except for the minor rap sheet. All the murders were a clean get-a-way.

He played the victim in public because he came from a broken home, as they used to say. Today it would be from a dysfunctional family. Either way he also was a nut job. Payne loved to start trouble among his co-workers at Cimarron Technologies. It didn't matter what it was, he'd start trouble. Once he had complained to his supervisor that a coworker, Sharon got the easy work and the best machine and he didn't simply because she was a woman. After a confrontation with management and the union he eventually won out, got the job and the machine.

Most people were afraid of him so they gave him a wide berth. They would have given him a wider berth if they knew his real past. If the police knew about him they would call him a serial killer. His modus operandi was he would use a gun to kill men and a knife for women. A knife was personal, and he got to be very personal with five women on his journey through the years to Oklahoma

City. With each of his female victims he would cut a cross between their breasts with his knife. The men received a final shot up the anus. He never deviated. If the police departments of the different states ever synchronized, they would profile him as hating both men and women—anti-social.

He didn't keep friends long. Angie worked next to him at the plant and because of his smooth talk, and curly hair, she took a shine to him. She didn't know about his past, the violence, the peeking at young girls and women, the molestations and their deaths. On their second date she learned about his five ex-wives. Drinking heavily and drunk, he let it slip about his ex's. The heavy drinking and the ex-wives were too much for her. She told him he was a piece of shit and dumped him like a truck load of crap. Payne never let go and he wanted back in her life. Maybe he could consummate the relationship this time. But she had changed departments and avoided him like a bad omen.

Payne reached his house at dusk and pulled his truck into the one bay garage. He walked to the spare bedroom where he kept his guns. The law or convictions couldn't stop him from having guns. He could always get guns or drugs or most anything else illegally.

Taking out a Beretta .380, he sat at a table and began to clean it. He opened a bottle of Hoppe's cleaning solvent, dipped the cotton patch in it and ran it down the barrel. Slowly at first, then he pulled the rod out. He put it back in, faster. In and out, going faster thinking of Angie. Breathing heavy he laid the tool down and went over to the closet. Payne pulled down a shoebox from the shelf. The box held his most prized possessions, photos. The pictures were marked with the names of every woman he had sex with, including his ex-wives and prostitutes. The dates were under the names of each woman. Except for one woman he never made it with. Smiling he reached for Angie's photo. Picking it up he licked his lips. Staring intently at her image he thought soon he would have her. He wanted her badly.

23

June 23; 6 P.M.

After Angie's near death beating at the hands of her former psycho boyfriend, John, Lance drilled a small hole into her front door, and installed a fisheye lens at her eye level for security purposes. Hearing a knock Angie jumped, still edgy after the attack. She peeked through the lens and saw Ronnie standing there. Angie opened the door and squealed with delight. She grabbed Ronnie and hugged her. Homer came running up and stood on his hind feet, tail wagging. Ronnie looked down.

"Oh, how cute. You have a...mutt."

The dog barked. Ronnie bent and petted him.

"Yes, but he can be a pest. Homer, go lie down."

Dejected, Homer left.

"I'm so happy you're here Ronnie. It's so good to see you."

"Look at you, girl. You're all grown up." It had been a muggy day and sweat rolled off her lip.

"Yeah, I'm not thirteen any longer." She squeezed Ronnie again. "You haven't changed a bit."

"I've aged some. I'm not twenty-two anymore." They giggled.

Ronnie asked, "What's with all the scars and bruises? How are you?"

"I'm okay, just got out of the hospital yesterday. You wouldn't believe what has happened to me."

"That's why you didn't answer your phone. I thought maybe you were at work."

"No. I got home late, picking up some groceries."

"When you wrote you said you needed a friend you could trust I thought I'd come here, get a job, and help you. I came by earlier but no answer."

"I was at the Mall then. I'm so glad you came. Here, sit down. Do you want something to eat or drink?"

"Thanks, I'll take a beer if it's no trouble."

"No trouble at all."

While Angie got the beer, Ronnie looked around her house. She noticed everything was clean and perfect. *How does she do this?* Angie's house measured about 1200 square feet. In the living room Ronnie sat on a white crushed velvet sofa. Catty-corner from her, by the bay window, sat a matching chair. The fireplace had dried flowers on the mantle. A 32" Sony Trinitron TV graced an area across from the sofa and chair. The small dining room contained a polished oak table and four chairs. Off the dining room was a small kitchen that Angie fished two beers out of the icebox, as she called it.

She handed Ronnie her 3.2 Coors from the grocery store, sat, and said, "I'm so glad you're here."

"You keep saying that." She smiled.

"How did you get here? By plane or bus?"

"My Harley."

"You got here all the way from Phoenix on a motorcycle?"

"I like to travel light."

"Girl, you're tough."

"I do okay."

"Well, I'm not. I've been having some problems with a couple of men."

"You've always had problems with men, hon. I wish I had your problems with them."

"No you don't. Seems like I always attract weirdos. I wish I could find someone worthwhile."

"Yeah, I know what you mean."

"Really. After I date them awhile, they show their true colors and I dump them. But they don't want to leave. They start stalking me."

"You poor thing. What do you do about that?" She drank her beer while she listened.

"I told the police but they can't do anything. My good friend, Lance and my former boyfriend, Mike, helped me with the last one. He was a real creep." She took a long pull of her beer. "They had to kill him."

"What!" Ronnie spit some beer out.

"The cops couldn't do anything…well, I did tell them that he raped me."

"My gosh, Angie!"

"The cops couldn't find the creep after that. Then the creep followed me Monday and my friends followed us but we didn't know it. They showed up just in time and it turned ugly. Lance had to shoot him."

"How awful." Ronnie had put her beer down and sat on the edge of the couch.

"Now someone tore up my cacti out back."

"What? Who would do that?"

"I think it might be a jerk I used to work with."

"Are you afraid of him?"

"Yes. I'm always scared. Would you come live with me? I have room. You can pay only a third of the mortgage payments to help me out. That would be your rent. Please say yes."

Ronnie held her eyes steady on Angie. She picked up her beer and drank half of it. Wiping her lips, she spoke, "Gee, girl, I don't mind living with you, but…"

Interrupting, Angie said, "You can also be my bodyguard so to speak. You won't have to be with me all of the time, just when I'm home or we go shopping or something like that."

"Gee, I'm not that tough."

"I know you're good with a gun and you can get your conceal carry license here after you've lived in the state for six months."

Ronnie didn't say anything right away. She was shocked and flattered. It was true that she knew how to handle weapons since she took a NRA course. She asked, "Why don't you get your license to carry?"

"I really don't like guns and I don't want to be responsible for someone's death. I've never shot a gun before but I've been around them. They're alright for whoever wants one. I don't think I'll ever be able to use one."

"Let me think about it. I just got here Wednesday late, and I have to start my new job Monday. The living part sounds good since I'm staying at a motel now. But the bodyguard stuff is scary. What about Lance, can't he be your bodyguard?"

"He owns three jewelry stores that keep him busy. I know he has his license and knows how to use a gun but he has other responsibilities. I don't want to strain my relationship with him by pressuring him to guard me all the time."

"Oh Angie, if you like him it's best to keep him close," she said smiling. "Anyway, I better go to pack up. And it's eight o'clock. Need some sleep, have to get up early. I have an appointment with Lance tomorrow, thanks to you." She smiled again. "I'd rather work at a jewelry store than a sand pit office."

"Good. I know you'll love working for him. I wish you would stay longer tonight."

"Love to, but I have things to pack at the motel."

"Thanks for coming."

"Hey, this is going to be an experience."

They hugged each other.

24

June 23, 8:30 P.M.

Angie spied Lance coming up the sidewalk and had the front door opened. He kissed her on the forehead as he went in.

"Woof! Woof!"

Lance saw a black mutt charging for him, then circling him.

"Isn't he cute? You finally get to meet Homer."

"Yeah, cute." *Why do women always have to have a pet?*

"What's the matter, don't you like Homer?"

"Oh, he's alright. At least he's not too big."

"Do you have a pet?"

"No, I don't have time to care for a pet."

Homer took off around the corner. A few seconds later he came trotting back with a ball and dropped it at Pruitt's feet.

"Aw, he likes you. He wants to play ball."

Why doesn't he hate me and leave me alone? I'm here for you. "What do I do with the ball?"

"Toss it, silly. He loves to play ball."

Lance tossed it around the corner. Homer tore off like a shot. It took him three seconds to bring it back. After a few minutes Lance was tired of the game so he pretended to throw the ball but the dog stood his ground.

Smart ass dog. "I'm having a lot of fun playing with your dog but I came here to visit you."

"Okay, you've been a good sport. Homer, go lie down."

Amazingly the dog obeyed. Lance caught a black object out of the corner of his eye coming cautiously toward him.

"Hi, Smokey. Do you want to meet Lance?"

"Aw, she's a little thing."

The cat walked up to him and sniffed him. He let her.

"Smokey likes you too."

Lance reached down and petted her. "How do you know?"

"She has her tail straight up."

"The question is, do you like me?"

"You know I do." Her cheeks flushed a muted red.

"I'm glad your pets like me and I like black cats. They have a good personality. But I'd like to know you better. I think you are so beautiful."

She smiled at him.

"And smart," he continued. "You are a smart woman."

"That doesn't scare you?"

"Why should it? I have confidence in myself. Plus, a smart woman should make life easier."

"Would you like some wine?"

"I'd love some."

"From the living room he watched her take a wine bottle out of the refrigerator. She laid it on the counter top and picked two wine glasses out of the cupboard.

For a moment Pruitt envisioned her in a carnal coupling with nut job Cunningham, whose taxi license photo had been in the newspaper announcing his demise. Lance was repulsed by the image and himself for imagining it. He knew his image wasn't true, except for the crime John committed. Fact of the matter, John was in Hell, no ands, ifs, or buts. That's worse than life in prison. So, everything was cool. Unless one didn't believe in God.

She came in carrying the bottle in one hand and the two glasses in the other. Lance reached for the bottle.

"Here. Let me pour."

They each sipped the wine and Angie said, "You just missed Ronnie."

"Oh. I'm sorry I did."

"She had to go back to the motel and get ready for tomorrow."

After a couple of glasses, Lance found himself sitting next to her. After a few moments she leaned into him and he kissed her. After they parted, they gazed into each other's eyes smiling. Then Lance reached for her and they kissed passionately. Emotion trumps everything, good or bad.

25

Saturday, June 24

One red eye opened slowly. It looked at the digital clock on the nightstand. It told the eye it was six thirty in the morning. Lance moaned. He turned off the alarm before it was supposed to go off. He didn't want to go to work but that's what happens when you're the boss. Plus, he promised Angie to meet with Ronnie.

Slowly rolling out of bed, he yawed, stretched and walked to the bathroom. He looked at himself in the mirror. The reflected face was unshaven and his hair looked like a flock of chickens ran through it. He picked up his razor and shaved. Even with shaving cream the razor felt like fingernails scraping across his face. After his shower, Lance poured almond "milk" over a bowl of fruit and fiber cereal. He threw a handful of vitamins into his mouth and washed them down with a big gulp of apple juice. After he brushed his teeth, that finished his morning ritual.

He strolled into the garage, set the alarm to the house, and opened the garage door. Today he decided to drive his new 2000 Corvette, bright red with black interior and a six speed. The engine roared to life as he turned the key. The dash clock said 8:04. He slowly backed it out of the garage.

One mile later he drove it slowly through Dry Creek, the small town he called home. He didn't want to disturb his neighbors—or the police. Travelling north on US 81 the Corvette easily reached the 65-mph speed limit on the two-lane highway.

Lance muttered, "I hope one day they'll widen this road."

Ten minutes after leaving his house, Lance glided onto I-40 and travelled east. He eased the 'Vette to 75 mph, set the cruise control and enjoyed the drive to his store on Penn Avenue.

At nine o'clock Ronnie Tanner would meet him there. Ronnie was waiting for him when he pulled into his parking place.

"Good morning," he said cheerfully.

"Good morning, Mr. Pruitt." She had to giggle, she felt so good. She wore a navy-blue skirt that came three inches above her knees. A white short sleeve blouse with small ruffles that lined her neck and came to a vee where her cleavage began. Her navy-blue shoes with stacked heels added two inches to her five feet six-inch height.

"I love your car, Mr. Pruitt."

"Thank you, Ronnie."

Ronnie loved the smile he gave her.

"It's beautiful." Ronnie smiled back.

"Thanks again. I like it."

Lance unlocked the door and led her to his office. The employees would be arriving soon.

"Wow, this is nice."

"I'm glad you like it. Have a seat." He pointed to two chairs that were facing each other with a coffee table between them.

"Thanks." Ronnie scanned the office. "Good, you have a computer. I'm pretty good with them. This one seems different though. I know it's not an Apple or a Microsoft type."

He went to his desk and laid his briefcase on top. He looked over at Quark. "Oh, that's Quark. It's got a ton of memory and has many other things it can do. As you can see it's not that much larger than a regular desk top." Lance went on to explain to Ronnie how Quark worked.

"That's really cool, Lance. I love the flat panel for the screen. Is it heavy?"

"The screen? No."

Lance got back on track. "Angie told me you needed to talk with me and that you are a friend of hers. That you need a place to stay." He walked over to the empty chair and sat.

"Yes. I feel like a beggar, but I don't know anyone who could help me find a place. I didn't ask Angie, cause she has her problems. She did ask me though… to stay…with her. She also told me about the stalking. This is why I wanted to talk with you. About Angie, a job, and some place to live."

"I will do anything I can for Angie, or her friend." Lance lowered his voice. "So, you don't have a job here?"

"I'm supposed to start with Dolese this coming Monday."

"Would you consider working for me here?"

Ronnie didn't really expect that even though Angie had mentioned it. Her heart started to race. She didn't know why. He's not only a man, but a handsome and rich one. She stumbled over her words.

"Yeah, yes. Sure."

"That's taken care of then. I'll call Dolese for you and explain that I stole you away."

Lance crossed-four his legs and put a hand on his knee. He thought she looked very sexy in her skirt. He liked what he saw.

"I have an extra bedroom at my house that you could stay in and have the run of the house…until you find a more permanent place. Is this agreeable with you?"

She was so taken aback that all she could do was nod her head in the affirmative with her mouth gaping like a cave. She had forgotten about Angie's offer.

"Now that you are taken care of is there anything else I can help you with?"

Then the cave spoke. "Uh, yes. Uh." She hesitated a few seconds and caught her wits. "Angie invited me to stay with her."

"That's better yet. You'd be closer to the store and right there with Angie, in case something happens. Uh, not that anything will."

"Well, Angie told me about a weirdo she thinks is watching her."

"Again?"

"I guess again."

"Who does she think it is?"

"A guy named Chad Payne—I think. He used to work with her at Cimarron Tech. Said he likes to start trouble with people. He's been stalking around her house when she was at work."

"She knows this, how?"

"A neighbor told her."

"That's good a neighbor is watching things. She hasn't told me." Lance seemed a little perturbed. *Quark had mentioned and updated his info of the other stalker, and named Chad Payne. So, that's the guy.*

Ronnie's face took on a pained expression. "Maybe she doesn't think you'll believe her."

"Believe her! I had to kill a bastard that was trying to kill her. And me for that matter."

Ronnie, surprised at his outburst, stammered, "I…I don't know, but she wants me to be her bodyguard. I told her I don't think so. At least that's what I wanted to tell her. But she seemed so scared. I don't know what to do."

"For one thing, after you've lived here for six months you can apply for your conceal carry license. In the meantime, I think you probably should stay with Angie."

"That's what Angie told me about applying for my gun license and she asked me to stay with her and you're right, I probably should do that. Could I still work for you?"

"The job is yours if you want it. It pays $320 a week."

"I'll take it. Thank you, Mr. Pruitt."

"Good. Now maybe you should go over and talk to Ange about living with her. If she can't have you room with her, my place will still be available. And please, call me Lance.

"Thanks again…Lance."

Ronnie stood and went over to him, bent over and kissed him on the cheek. "Thank you."

When she turned and walked out of the office, Lance thought that was a bold thing for her to do to her boss. He didn't really care, he liked it. Ronnie had a beauty that complimented her. Not as beautiful as Angie, but she was very pleasing to the eye. He felt good and good-looking women made him feel better.

The rest of the day at the store was profitable and Pruitt went home that evening a contented man.

26

June 24; 8 A.M.

Saturday morning dawned beautiful, a few billowing clouds, a slight breeze, so a good day to run. Angie usually ran in the evenings but it's been too hot lately. Dressed in pink shorts and a light green tank top, today she treated herself to a workout at Lake Hefner Trails. The bike and jogging paths were the best in Oklahoma City.

Driving her Honda, she took the Britton Road exit on Lake Hefner Parkway, crossed over the parkway and made a left. She drove past the restaurant and the sailboat harbor on the right. She pulled into the parking lot just beyond the sailboats.

Stretching first before jogging she took a deep breath and let it out. The morning warmed up quickly. Angie started jogging at an even pace. She loved the scenery bouncing by her, as her shoes hit the blacktop path. She glanced from time to time at the few sailboats on the lake and a couple of park benches along the way. The path headed for the wooded area starting with a few trees here and there, mostly pine and oak. Then the wooded area thickened on either side of her. By the time she reached the halfway point through the wooded section she had worked up a sweat. She slowed down to a brisk walk, then walking with her hands on her hips. She looked ahead and saw a specter.

Chad Payne parked his truck next to Angie's car. He strolled over to it to see if it was locked. It was. He looked south along the path. He didn't see her. Taking his binoculars out of the truck, he looked again. He spotted her this time. She was jogging at a steady pace and about seventy-five yards before she would enter the scanty woods. Chad jumped in his pickup and drove back onto Lake Hefner Parkway. He took the 63rd Street exit and headed to Meridian Avenue. He turned right into the park and found a spot for his truck. He walked to the end of the trail and waited for Angie.

He didn't have to wait long. Her youthful tight body walking towards him, titillating his eyes and every man's who saw her pass by.

Angie spied him one hundred yards away and stopped short. She coughed sucking in air.

He smiled and waved.

"Angie! I need to see you," he yelled.

He waved for her to come. She stood still, breathing steadily. Chad inched forward. Breathing in and out slowly, she observed him. Could she out run him back to the car? You bet. Angie turned and ran full tilt.

"Shit!"

Chad ran to his pickup. He tore off, tires screaming like hell on the pavement.

"Damn these lights. Come on, come on."

He caught every light. Gunning his engine didn't make the light change any quicker, but it got the attention of a passing cop. The light changed and he floored a left onto the ramp to the parkway. The cop spun around and tore off in hot pursuit.

"Shit!"

Chad became a model citizen and did not cause a problem with the officer. Acting up would destroy his chances of catching up to Angie.

"Since you said you're running late to visit your mother and you have no current warrants and seem to be keeping your nose clean, I'll just give you a warning."

"Thank you, officer. I really appreciate that."

"Drive carefully now."

"You bet I will."

After Chad received his warning ticket he drove over to where Angie had parked. Gone, of course. That damn flatfoot.

When Angie arrived at her house she immediately went to the phone.

"Witkowski. Homicide."

"This is Angie Tilghman. I hate to bother you but I have another stalker."

"Angie, this is no bother. Do you know who it is?"

"Yes. His name is Chad Payne."

"How old is he?"

"Around forty-six. I don't know why I dated him. He's a real creep. He told me he came from Kansas City."

"Kansas or Missouri?"

Angie hesitated. "I don't know."

Witkowski wrote everything down as she spoke. Angie gave Witkowski all the details she knew, as well as more personal rants. He then remembered Lance's computer giving that name, Chad Payne.

Witkowski asked her, "Do you know of any other men that you've been with that might be stalkers or acted like John or Payne?"

Angie was slow in answering. When she did she sounded upset.

"No. No one else has been crazy, except for John. And crazy Chad, who I also dumped. There haven't been many men in my life."

"Sorry to upset you but I have to know. Two men stalking you within a month is a little odd. As a matter of fact, I have never had a case like this before. So, I'm gathering information."

Witkowski told her that he would check everything out about Payne as a special favor to her since this wasn't a homicide case and she was out of his jurisdiction.

"Thank you, Lieutenant."

"It's Nick. I want you to be extremely careful when you are out and about."

"I will…Nick." She kept forgetting to call him by his first name. She was brought up to call older men by their titles and last names.

When they hung up, Witkowski got on his computer reluctantly and opened VICAP's site using the Oklahoma Police password authorized by the FBI, and typed with two fingers, Payne's name. The Violent Criminal Apprehension Program took about two minutes for Payne's name came up with a list of minor offenses, the assault and batteries, some thefts, and other minor reports. No currents. He lived in a rural part of South West Oklahoma City, west of Mustang, and owned a 1975 Chevy truck. Present employer was Cimarron Technologies.

His crimes were in four cities and states. Witkowski verified that he came from Kansas City, Kansas. Maryland was not included since Payne was not using that name there. As far as Witkowski knew his crimes started in Ohio. VICAP states his age then as twenty-three. Payne did give his birth as being in Baltimore. Very interesting.

Witkowski wondered about those missing years. No crimes committed in Maryland. Doesn't seem plausible. Unless he has a juvenile sheet. Witkowski hit print and three sheets of accordion paper printed. He left his office and walked over to Margaret's desk which held the old printer. He tore off the paper and returned to his desk. He signed off on the computer

He sat holding the print-out and studied it. He spun the O on the dial of his rotary phone.

"Yes, operator, I'd like to make a long-distance call to the Baltimore City Police Headquarters."

"I can give you the direct number."

"Okay."

"Four-one-oh, five, five, five, seven, two, one, two."

"Thanks."

"I thought she'd do it for me," he said aloud to no one.

It wasn't an emergency so he spun the dial eleven times.

"Baltimore City police, Sargent Kolodziejski."

Witkowski was speechless for a few seconds. "Are you related to Ed?"

"Yes. Who's this?"

"Nick Witkowski with Oklahoma City Police. How are you related to Ed?"

"I'm his son, Bob. I've heard about you."

"Good, I hope."

"It is. You know dad's retired?"

"I didn't know but I thought he might be. He used to be my supervisor."

"Yeah, he told me what happened in your rookie year. I'm glad I'm talking to you. You almost bought the farm."

Witkowski was silent for a moment.

"Yeah, and I never had the chance to pay that killer for it."

Bob cleared his throat. "Well, what can I do for you, Nick?"

"I need to speak to someone who can help me with juvie records."

"That would be Lieutenant Smith. I'll transfer you. Great talking with you Nick."

"Same here. Thanks. And say hi to your dad for me."

"Will do."

Witkowski heard a couple of clicks, then nothing, then, "Lieutenant Smith."

"Lieutenant, this is Lieutenant Witkowski with Oklahoma City Police and I was hoping you could help me track someone."

"Glad to help. Whatcha got?"

"I need a juvenile record on a Chad Payne, P-A-Y-N-E."

"Well, you know those are sealed."

"Would you be able to tell me, without opening the record, if Chad Payne's name is on any juvie?"

"How old would he be now and would this be a capital crime?"

"He's around forty-five to forty-seven and he hasn't committed any capital crime that we know of. But we do have a big problem with him and it could get bigger."

"Hold on, let me check our computer records."

While Witkowski was holding Margaret came in and asked him if he wanted coffee.

"Yes, black. Thanks."

Margaret brought in a ceramic cup with the OKC Police badge on it. He took a sip and jumped. Too hot.

"Still there?"

"Yeah, I'm here."

"I don't think this will help but there is no one with that name. That we have."

"Crap. If I sent you a set of prints would that help?"

"Yes. We take prints off of every one of them."

"Okay. I don't have the prints yet but I'll get them somehow."

"I'll be waiting. By the way my name is John."

"Oh, one of those."

"Yes, I'm afraid."

"Mine's Nick."

"Now I recognize the name. Sounds like you're doing okay."

"I am, thanks. And I'll be doing better when I get the subjects' prints."

They hung up and Witkowski thought about, how would he get those prints?

27

June 25

itkowski awoke early Sunday morning. He had a tough time sleeping, thinking about Chad Payne, after Angie's call yesterday. It was bad when he dreamed about him—that kept him tossing and turning. He left his house at seven without breakfast. He drove north on Santa Fe Avenue heading for headquarters. He looked to his right as he passed by the Santa Fe Briefing Station, the place he worked until he transferred to Central. Every day that he passed by, he said, "Smooth sailing," and continued toward Central.

Witkowski was going to find more info on Payne. He needed the computers at headquarters to do a proper job.

Homicide was empty when he got there as he knew it would be. He sat at Margaret's desk and booted her computer. He went on the OTC site for police and found Payne's address. He wrote it down. Then he went into VICAP again and typed in Payne's name. He used Margaret's note pad and wrote down the cities and states that Payne had a record. He noted the months and years he lived in each city. He started to write all the information he thought pertinent. Then, he thought, *Come on Witty, you can print this stuff.* He hit print.

Witkowski reached the printer and waited until it finished. He picked up eight accordion pages of Payne's sheet.

He said to no one, "I wish they'd get us one of the new type printers." Taking everything to his office he dropped the sheets on his desk.

"Crap", he said and went back to Margaret's desk and logged out and turned off the computer. He limped to his desk and sat. Next, he separated the pages and put them in order. Then he read page one. He noticed Payne spent less than five years in each city. Payne was consistently moving west with each new move, finally arriving in Oklahoma City probably in ninety-seven or ninety-eight. He checked Payne's age and figured that he left Baltimore when he was twenty-two or three. That would be around 1976 and no record of him in Baltimore. Strange. Unless he changed his name and had a juvie record that was his real name. John Smith said there was no record for a Chad Payne. He'd ask Kansas City to send him Payne's prints. With most of these charges against him they should have his prints. He'll do that first thing tomorrow.

Reading about Payne, Witkowski knew this mutt was capable of doing worse than his record showed. Most stalkers were psychotic killers. Somehow, he had to put him away for good.

Nick decided to pay Payne a visit and pushed his chair back slightly, opening his bottom right drawer. Lifting his Smith and Wesson 1911 SC .45 ACP he checked the magazine; it was fully loaded with seven rounds. Then he jacked a round and released the magazine. Again, he reached into his desk drawer, grabbed another round out of the box and slid it into the clip and slammed the ammo back into the pistol. Engaging the safety, since now it was ready to fire, he slipped the weapon into its holster which left the original wood grip exposed. Unbuckling his belt, he slid it through the holster and tightened it. He left his office and signed out a panda scout car. Once in a while he called the black and whites, pandas, after he heard a detective friend in Los Angeles call their cars pandas.

Witkowski decided to go alone this time since it was a Sunday and he didn't plan on arresting Payne. Just ask him questions, and maybe put the fear of the Oklahoma City Police Department in him. The main reason was that he didn't want any witnesses in case things went south.

Witkowski drove west on I-40 until he got off at the Czech Hall Road exit. He headed south until he spotted SW 27th Street and made a right. He saw number 411635 and pulled onto the long gravel driveway to the house. Luck was with Nick; Payne's truck was in the driveway. He didn't think Payne was a church person. Witkowski pulled in behind the truck.

Payne lived in Oklahoma City but with a Yukon address. The small manufactured house looked fairly nice. The landlord probably kept it up. All the other houses had a good amount of space between them and Payne's was no exception.

Nick rolled out of his vehicle and limped to the door. He knocked hard and fast like a machine gun, as he does when he's serving a warrant.

Payne jerked the door open. "What the hell do you want?"

"Chad Payne?"

Sneering he said, "Yeah, what do you want I said."

Witkowski thought, *we're off to a good start*. He badged him and said, "I'm Detective Witkowski, Oklahoma City. I would like to talk to you. May I come in?"

"What's it about? I dint do nothin.'"

"I didn't say you did. Can I step in and we talk?"

Payne eyed him suspiciously but backed away to let him in.

"Thank you." Nick looked around and saw that a sofa and two stuffed chairs faced each other in the middle of the room. You had to walk behind the furniture to get to the other parts of the small house. He picked a chair. "This will do. Sit…please."

Payne walked to the couch, sat, leaned back with his arms stretched across the back and crossed his legs. They stared at each other for a few seconds. Witkowski moved his eyes from him and looked around the living room. No pictures on the walls, a small lamp table and lamp with a torn shade, no homey feel, just a sofa and the two stuffed chairs. He noticed that the arms on the chairs were worn threadbare. He brought his eyes back to Payne. He had on a dirty white tee shirt with a couple of holes and faded blue jeans, ripped at the knees. No shoes. Witkowski could tell a lot about a person by the way they lived. Sitting there he couldn't come up with a plan for getting prints, so he came to shake things up. He looked Payne in the eye and spoke.

"You know Angie Tilghman, right?"

"Yeah. So what?"

"She tells me you are bothering her and possibly stalking her."

"She's full of shit. I ain't stalking her butt. We're friends and I just wanted to talk to her. It's still a free country, ain't it?"

"Sure is. But this country also has laws against stalking."

"I toll you man, I ain't stalking her ass."

"Okay, let me put it like this. If she calls me again about you, I'll put your ass in jail for stalking, vagrancy, spitting on the sidewalk, and a couple of other things that will take a public defender a lot of time to go through before, or if, he can get you out on bail. That means you will go to trial. And the Oklahoma City jail isn't too comfy."

They stared at each other. Payne broke first by shifting his eyes to the right and behind Witkowski. Witkowski warned, "Better thought, I will file state charges for stalking."

"I ain't stalking her, man. I don't even like the stuck-up bit…"

He stopped talking, watching Witkowski's finger wag side to side.

"If you are going to lie, Payne, have the decency to be good at it. Just remember what I said."

Payne glared at Witkowski. Then, "I hear you, man. Thanks for the warning."

Nick stood. "I can find my way out." He tried not to limp too much.

Chuckling he yelled, "Hey, gimpy, tell Angie I love her."

Witkowski stopped, spun around, reached the couch Payne sat on, in what seemed like two seconds, grabbed him by the non-existing lapels of his funky tee shirt and yanked his six-foot frame up. Their noses were four inches apart with Witkowski looking up into Payne's face.

"It was a scumbag like you that gave me the limp. He got away, but you can take his place. If you so much as get within two miles of Angie and I hear about it, I'll do more than give *you* a limp."

He shoved Payne hard, back onto the sofa. Payne and the couch fell on their backs.

Witkowski didn't stop or look back, he just shut the door gently. Outside he heard Payne yell, "I oughta sue your ass, gimp. Police brutality and harassment. I'll sue the whole shitin' police department, you gimpy bastard!"

Witkowski smiled getting into the car. He felt good as he drove towards home—though the gimpy part hurt.

On the way he stopped at a seven eleven and bought a coffee. He sat in the car awhile and thought. Nick knew Payne was big trouble but how to stop him was the problem. Well, staying within the law was the problem.

"That damn Witkowski bracing me." Payne was worried but not enough to stop. "I can handle him…or avoid him. At least I know what I'm up against."

He lifted his couch upright and said, "I'll get him for this."

28

Monday, June 26; 7:30 A.M.

It was the best of times; it was the worst of times…
The words of Charles Dickens crept into Lance's mind, stealthily as a cat. The mewing of the words kept haunting him. He knew the truth of those words for him. There was once a love of his life that made his life a living hell. He had wanted with all his heart that their lives together would be heaven. At those times, he had found himself trying to breathe life into a relationship that had used up all its nine lives. Now he thought that maybe the best of times was approaching. The chemistry was there—maybe. Lance couldn't put his finger on it, but it was there. The feeling of joy when he was with Angie. Now he was coming to her aid. His feelings toward Angie were growing. He had tried to fight them off. Why?

"Stupidity." He said out loud.

No, not that. Maybe, once burned, twice shy. Or fear of rejection.

"No, I don't fear rejection. What's my problem?"

At the same time, he realized that dating her would answer a plethora of questions. Like would she be good for him and vice versa. At least his biological clock wasn't running out. He smiled.

Lance was on his way to Angie's house. She had previously called him in a panic and she didn't have to ask him twice. He had dropped everything and left right away. Proving that his feelings for her had swelled. So, a half an hour after leaving his house Pruitt arrived at hers.

Parking the Corvette in her driveway, he rolled out and rang the doorbell. Angie answered the door wearing a royal purple mini skirt, lightweight white sweatshirt, and barefoot.

Man, she's gorgeous. His heart jumped. *Show your feelings man.*

"Thanks for coming. You always come to my rescue. And that's been a lot lately."

"No problem."

She smiled.

"What's up?"

"There's a guy watching me."

"Again? Like how? Who?"

"He follows me and comes to the house when I'm not here."

"Is Ronnie living with you yet?"

"Tomorrow."

"Do you know this guy?"

"Yes. His name is Chad Payne. I used to work with him and just dated him twice. I called Detective Witkowski Saturday and told him about Chad. Am I being paranoid this time?"

"A wise man once said, it isn't paranoia if they really *are* out to get you."

"I think he is then."

"Yeah, Ronnie said as much. She filled me in with a couple of details. I'm glad you told Nick."

Angie added, "He said he would have a talk with Chad."

"Oh, boy." Lance grunted. *Sometimes that really ticks some guys off.* He remembered Quark telling him about Chad Payne.

The doorbell rang. Angie opened the door.

"Hi, Angie."

"Come in. We were talking about you."

"I hope it was good. Hi, Lance."

"Hi, Ronnie," Lance said smiling.

"I came over to ask you if I can bring my stuff over today instead of tomorrow?" Ronnie asked with some trepidation.

"Sure thing. I'd be glad to have you here sooner." Angie sounded relieved. She didn't want to admit to them that she was more scared and worried than she let on about having a gun in the house. "I've never shot a gun or really know how to fight effectively. I probably could use a gun if push came to shove."

"I'll give you some pointers. My dad taught me. I grew up with them," Ronnie said.

"You Arizonians have guts and guns," Lance said.

"Thanks, Lance. So do you Oklahomans."

"I feel safe with Ronnie…at least safer. But Ronnie can't be with me twenty-four/seven."

"That's something we need to think about," Lance interjected. "When you're at work, Ronnie, Angie will not be protected by you or me. She might be watched by Chad boy. So, Angie, I want you to keep your eyes open all the time. Be constantly aware of your surroundings."

"I do. I am." Angie said not trying to hide the hurt. "At work it's okay."

"I'm not trying to insult you. I mean you really have to keep them open when you're not at work. Always be aware of what's going on around you and near you. I know it's tough to live like that, but right now it's very necessary. We don't know what he's up too…yet," Lance warned.

He sat on the sofa and in a gentler tone he continued, "If he does anything you don't like, I want both of you to call me on my cell phone and let me know right away. I'm not going to play with him. I'll set him up if I have to, to get him to stop, or to get rid of him."

The two women gazed at him and then at each other. Fear on Angie's face, apprehension on Ronnie's.

"Okay." Angie said.

"I've got to be going. You ladies take care."

He kissed Angie on the forehead and shook Ronnie's hand with both of his. He backed the 'Vette out of the driveway and headed for store number two in the south part of town on South Western Avenue.

29

Tuesday, June 27; 7 A.M.

Lance woke up smiling. With the dream about Angie fresh in his memory, he felt closer to her, love in his heart. He had over slept. So what, it was worth it. He reached for the phone and dialed Angie's number.

"Hello."

"Did I wake you up?"

"No. I've been up. Lance, this is you, isn't it?"

"Yes. I was wondering if I could come over and see you now?"

"Is something the matter? Is it Chad?"

"No. I'd like to talk to you. That's all. If it's inconvenient…"

"No. You can come over."

"Great. I'll be there in an hour."

Lance hung up elated. Forty minutes later he was travelling north on US 81. He felt good. The morning sun warmed his skin at the same time the wind cooled him. The cloudless horizon beckoned him. He scanned to his left and right; brown fields had been harvested of their wheat. Some of the fields had been disked. Groups of trees stood here and there like curious onlookers. Twenty minutes away Angie waited.

He guided the Vette onto her driveway. Walking to her door he pushed the key fob and locked the car. Lance took a deep breath and rang her bell. The door opened and Angie stood there smiling at him.

She always looks so beautiful. Lance smiled. That was all he could do. His feet were glued to the stoop.

"Come in. Or do you want to stand out there all day?"

"No. I mean yes. Ah, no."

Angie giggled. He came in and she pointed to the sofa.

"Sit down, Lance. Now what do you have on your mind?"

He sat next to her.

Nervously he said, "I'd like to ask your opinion about, ah about if, well have you ever wanted someone and known that person is no good for you then have that person prove to you they're not good for you. Then you get rid of that person and still you want that person?" He paused and studied his hands. "I had a woman like that, she was terrible for me and to me. It's taken a long time for me to get her out of my system. To this day, I wish it could have been normal, or as normal as possible, with her. Weird. I do miss her. I did miss her. But something has changed." He looked at her.

Angie studied him as if he had six eyes. "What are you talking about or who?"

"My feelings toward you."

Lance stared at the wall with a look that made Angie's heart ache with desire.

"Lance, I'm here." She rested her hand on the sofa.

He reached for her hand, took it, and kissed it. Angie trembled as his face lifted to meet hers. He leaned over and kissed her softly on the lips. Lance smiled. Angie threw her arms around him and kissed him hard. He would be late getting to his store.

Payne slowly cruised SW 13th Street heading toward Tilghman's house. When he got closer, he spied a new Corvette in her driveway.

"Now who the hell is that?"

He found a spot to park his truck two houses away where he could keep an eye on the Vette. He debated with himself whether to stay or get out. He decided to get out. Looking around he didn't see any neighbors. Everything looked buttoned up. He glanced at his watch: 9:36. Probably all at work. Walking in front of his truck he froze. He heard a man and Angie talking, coming from her house.

He's leaving, registered in his brain. He hurried around his truck and jumped in. He closed the door silently. Then he saw a man turn back to the house and wave. *Who's that turd? It ain't that puke, Mike.* He crouched low in the seat, then he had to drop his head. The rumbling of the Vette made him smile. He would pay Angie a visit.

The Vette finally left. Payne was about to get out of the truck when he saw a police car in the rear-view mirror, patrolling the neighborhood.

"Shit." He ducked again. He stayed that way for at least three minutes. Poking his nose up then his eyes, he saw that the coast was clear. Too Close. Time for him to leave. It had been an Oklahoma City black and white scout car. *Damn Witkowski.*

30

Saturday, July 1, 7:30 A.M.

Chad Payne jumped into his truck and drove to south Oklahoma City. The radio said it was going to be over 100 degrees again. For over three weeks the temperature rose above, as the weathermen say, the century mark. Payne cursed the heat. Already it reached eighty-seven. He hated the burning sun on his skin when it went over 106. One hundred was bad enough, but over 106 it had a burning sensation. The land showed the effects of the long heat and drought. One of these days he would leave this city for good and he'd have Angie with him. For now, heat or not, he was going to get some crank.

He swung over to the May Avenue exit off I-240 and drove the service road until he came to the correct apartment complex. Payne pulled into a spot. The weight of the Beretta against his leg felt comforting. His pants were baggy enough to hide it.

Payne climbed the steps and knocked on the door. A fat Hispanic woman cracked the door and peeked at him through a two-inch opening.

"Joe sent me."

She shut the door and undid the chain. He walked through the opening scanning left and right. Three dirt bags were lounging on a sofa, stoned.

"Want twenty-five dollars," Payne said.

Meth was often carried in a folded notebook paper or dollar bills, called "bindles."

The fat woman got the drug. He paid her. She handed the bindle to Payne. Sticking it in his back pocket, he backed out. Payne left, and drove back to his house with the stash.

The illegal drug crank, also known as speed, meth, and crystal meth, can be smoked, snorted, or taken orally.

Payne smoked his and took his pipe and sat in his easy chair. He placed the rock into the bowl of the pipe and lit it. In a short time, he felt like the Man of Steel, thinking himself as untouchable. The Meth heightened his paranoia, anger, pleasure, all his emotions, good or bad.

Payne had been using crank for a month and already began losing weight. Within a year, a crank user will have lost some teeth, if not all of them.

It was easy to get crank, or crack, in Oklahoma City and in the year 2000 the city ranked #1 in the nation for per capita meth lab busts. Crank users caused a lot of domestic violence and Payne was not immune. Every one of his marriages had been abusive even though he wasn't using often during those times. When a wife couldn't take it anymore, she'd leave but not without a fight. It took them awhile to leave because of his threats.

Methamphetamine, a highly additive stimulant, affects the brain with long term changes associated with impaired memory and motor coordination. Chemists had been perfecting it since the early nineteen hundreds. Sleeping sickness and extreme cases of obesity were treated with amphetamines in the nineteen-thirties. The doses were 2.5 to 15 milligrams per day. Payne felt meth made him better than he already was since it was used by German soldiers in World War II to keep them alert for battle. He felt it brought him closer to being a soldier himself. But he consumed 500 to 1000 milligrams at once to trigger his physical and psychological exhilarations. Today's crank users consume up to 1000 milligrams every three hours.

The outlaw biker gang, Hell's Angels did speed in the nineteen-sixties. Payne had started with speed to be like the Hell's Angels.

Payne didn't belong to the Hell's Angels but he now acted like one. He left the house, jumped into his truck and roared off towards "downtown" Yukon. He stopped at the bowling alley on Main Street. It was after nine in the evening when he stormed through the doors. Inside and off to his right was a lounge separated from the alleys proper. He sat down at the bar and ordered a whiskey. The shot disappeared in one gulp. Payne ordered another and after that vanished in two seconds, he ordered, "Hit me again."

"Aren't you drinking that a little too fast, my friend?" the bartender asked as he poured another shot.

Payne grabbed him by the collar. "What's it to you, asshole. Just pour."

"Get off of me or I'll call the police."

Payne pushed him back and the bartender fell into the bottles on the shelf behind him. Bottles bounced off the floor with the bartender, some breaking. The resident strong arm rushed up to Payne. Payne smashed him across the face with the bottle he drank from. The barkeep managed to call 911 as Payne downed some more whiskey from the bottle he used on strong arm. He headed for the lanes. Most of the bowling had stopped, people were observing what happened.

Payne pushed a man out of the way who was about to bowl, grabbed a ball and threw it shot put style down the alley. Next, he walked over to a woman and put his arm around her waist. She struggled to free herself which made Payne angrier. A man put his hand on Chad's shoulder and got punched in the face for his heroics. Most people started to clear out. Payne looked up from the fallen man and saw two Yukon cops hurrying towards him with their tactical batons in their hands. With a flick of their wrists the batons snapped to full length.

"Come on, boys. I'm ready."

The cops charged, swinging. Payne ducked the first one but ran into the second. The baton hit him below the left ear. He went down, then the first baton officer hit him on top of the head.

The last thing Payne remembered was laying on the floor looking at shiny black shoes.

The two arresting officers had him under each arm and dragged him into the Yukon police station on South Ranchwood Boulevard. They took him to a cell right away and dumped him. They walked back to the front to process him. The processing officer ask for his name, birth, other info, and what happened.

"Name's Payne and he sure is," officer Lee stated. "First name, Chad."

"Birth date's April thirtieth, nineteen fifty-four, a Taurus, and he acted like one," officer Leif informed the sergeant. He knew the sergeant consulted the astrological charts.

"The way he was acting and fighting he's probably on meth. Damn doper," Lee added.

Charges were, fighting, disturbing the peace, reckless behavior, endangering life, property damage, and assault on officers.

After the paperwork was finished L and L, as they were called, went back on patrol.

Payne went before a judge on Monday and received a month in jail and fined one thousand dollars for his night on the town. He was then transported to the Canadian County jail in El Reno to complete his sentence.

***

Four days into his stay at the county jail Payne in another moment of anger and indiscretion, bragged to his cell mate that he was a big shot and the cops didn't know it. No drugs to make him feel better, so he talked. Maybe even make him an ally.

"Hey, Cobb, whatcha in for?"

Cobb was about the same height and built as Payne. Younger, twenty-five, he looked forty.

"Possession of meth, man."

"Hell. That ain't nothin'. You in for a week?"

"Ten days." Cobb puffed up. "And for fighting."

"Yeah, well, they got me for fightin' and some other shit. I'm stuck here for a month."

Payne looked angrily at Cobb. "Let me tell you something, those bastards don't know who they have here. I've done worse shit and these pigs don't know it."

Payne gazed up and to the left chuckling. "Yeah, I've had some good times."

He looked at Cobb. "I was about your age, maybe younger, when I offed some prostitute. She was the first one to get my mark."

"Your mark?" Cobb questioned.

"Yeah. I carve a cross between their boobs." Payne seemed to study the wall.

Cobb stared at him with his mouth open showing a hole where a tooth should have been.

"That was in Baltimore. My first kill." He now had a faraway glaze. Shortly he came back. "Not long after that I killed some pigs who were after me. As you can see, they didn't get me." A satanic sound came out that was supposed to be laughter. "That was in seventy-six. What a good year."

Cobb still stared and swallowed.

"Yeah, I killed punks and hoes in Cincinnati and Kansas City too. The pigs never caught me. Dumb shits."

Cobb wanted to move away from this psycho but didn't want to upset him, so he didn't move.

"I showed all of them…don't fuck with me!" Payne barked.

Cobb jumped and moved. "Hey, man, cool it."

Payne glared at him, turned his back on him and laid on the metal bunk. He murmured, *pussy*.

Later after chow, on the way back to the cells, Cobb spoke low to a deputy. "I need to see the warden. I got info."

The deputy pointed and commanded, "Stand over there."

When everyone was gone from the cafeteria the deputy said, "There ain't no Warden sonny. Do you want to talk to the sheriff?"

"Sir, yes, sir."

Sheriff Mitchell Kinkade said. "What's on your mind. Cell too comfortable?"

"No sir, sheriff, it's fine. But my cell mate Chad, he toll me things and maybe if I toll you, you would get me out sooner."

"Doesn't work that way. But I could, maybe, make your stay more comfortable."

Cobb smiled. "Okay, sheriff. That's a deal."

The sheriff inspected the prisoner. "Let's just hear what you have first then we'll see."

"Chad toll me he's killed people."

"Why'd he tell you?"

"I dunno, but he was proud of it cause he said he never got caught."

"He said that?"

"Yes, sir, sheriff."

Sheriff Kinkade placed his hand on his bald head, thinking.

"Where were the murders? Did he say?"

"Yes, sir, he said Baltimore, Cincinnati, and I think Kansas City."

"Kansas or Missouri?"

"I dint know there was a Missouri City."

The sheriff let that slide. "Did he mention who he killed?"

"Only it was a prostitute and some cops. He carved a cross on the hooker's chest. He said it was in nineteen seventy-six."

The sheriff sat straight up. Payne might be more dangerous than he thought. He had thought to put him back with Payne to see what else he could get. No way now.

"I'm going to put you in a different cell. Don't tell him that you talked with me."

"Don't worry sheriff, I ain't stupid."

"Here you go sheriff, the update on Chad Payne." Deputy Glenda Morrison handed Kinkade the reports.

Kinkade looked at the papers and saw the added charge on it. The one he was in jail for now. There were no major felonies, mostly misdemeanors.

Was Payne just bragging about something he didn't do? Or did he do the murders and got away with it? If true, he was one dangerous hombre. He called his brother Jack, a State Trooper. The State had the same info on Payne. The Sheriff thought maybe the other states would have something on Payne. Kinkade sent out messages to the states mentioned by Payne and they all came back with the same thing Oklahoma City had on him. Baltimore City had no report on him before, during 1976, or after. Nothing about carved crosses on female chests. Kinkade let it go for now but he kept a close eye on him.

31

Friday, July 14

Witkowski twitched when his old phone rang. He had the ringer down but it still made a racket. Next to the old phone sat a touchtone phone he seldom used. He had that ringer off. "Detective Witkowski."

"Tessa Corbinelli, with *The Paseo* newspaper."

Witkowski sat up straight. "Yes, what can I do for you?"

"I hate to bother you but my editor wants me to do an article on the City police and I need a detective to complete the story."

He felt his face flush. "If you're asking if I would want to be interviewed, well, yes, you can interview me."

"This will only take a couple of minutes. Do you have the time?"

He looked at his watch. "It's almost lunchtime. Why don't you meet me at the front door and we'll go someplace close, have lunch and talk?"

"That sounds super. What time?"

"How about now?"

"It'll take me a little bit to get there."

"That's okay. When you get here have one of the officers behind the glass call me down."

"Okay. I'll be there shortly."

"See ya." Witkowski hung up elated. He hoped he didn't sound bossy or mean. He liked this girl, ah, woman, and he didn't want to blow it. He wondered how old she was, then he thought maybe he's too old. What of it? This is just a working lunch with a reporter. Still…

"Humph!"

He didn't see Margaret leaning against his door jam, with her arms folded.

"Yes, Margaret?" he questioned, sounding a little defensive.

"What's with the smile and the faraway look? Or maybe I should say, the spacy glaze."

"I wasn't spacy, I was thinking of the interview a reporter wants to take."

Still standing with her arms folded she said, "Of who?"

"What?"

"Of whom does she want to interview?"

"Me, Margaret, why?"

"Who's the reporter?"

"Uh, Tessa. Tessa Corbinelli. We're meeting for lunch."

"You old dog."

"What?"

She walked closer to his desk. "Here're the papers you wanted on the motorcyclist killed by the illegal alien." She put her hands on his desk and leaned in, smiling.

"You be careful. Those young women can warp your mind."

She turned and walked away. It took Witkowski a few seconds to recover.

"Are you jealous?"

She flapped her hand, reached her desk and sat. She didn't look at him but she was smiling, just to keep him confused.

He shook his head, stood, grabbed his Stetson, strode by her desk and informed her, "I'm going to lunch."

She watched him leave. "Have a good time."

Witkowski rode the elevator to the third floor where the sex crimes detectives were. He walked in and saw Art Morgan at his desk.

"Hey, Art, what's going on?"

"Hi, Nick. I got this weird setup. This woman was found face up, stabbed in the chest, stomach, and face forty-one times lying on her bed, all four limbs tied to the bed, duct tape across her mouth with the word, bitch, on it. The husband says he was in Phoenix. He came back today. And the boyfriend says he was home with his mother. I'm checking their alibis. The boyfriend looks solid but there is a slight anomaly."

"Boyfriend?"

"Yeah, one of those cases."

"When'd it happen?"

"Yesterday, last night. The coroner said time of death was between seven and eleven P.M. Whoever killed her was very, very, pissed."

"I'd say." Witkowski looked around. Only one other detective sat at his desk several yards away. He spoke low, "I want to ask you where's there a good restaurant close by to take a young lady reporter for lunch."

"I like Grand House on Classen. It's Chinese."

"Chinese is good. It'll be different for me. Thanks. And I hope you get whoever killed her."

"I hope so too. I think I will. Good luck with the reporter."

"Yeah, thanks. Good luck in finding the murderer."

"You're going to need the luck more than me," he laughed.

'Gee, thanks."

Taking the elevator down to the second floor he walked in the homicide office and asked Margaret if there was a call for him.

"Yes, two minutes ago. In the lobby. Where were you?"

"Upstairs. Hold down the fort."

He saw her before he stepped out of the elevator. His breath caught. He hoped it didn't show.

He took her hand in both of his. "My pleasure."

Out of the corner of his eyes he saw the two sergeants behind the glass snicker. He put his hand on Tessa's back to lead her out. He turned to the men. "Don't you two have paperwork to do?" Now they laughed.

Tessa said, "What's wrong with them?"

"Juveniles," he said. He didn't see, but Tessa was smiling.

In the lot across the street were police cars and their private vehicles. Nick approached a new 2000 white four door Buick.

"Nice car. I assume it's yours and not an undercover car."

"You assumed right. I bought it in March. Can't take the company's car for a joy ride."

"So, this is a joy ride?"

"Yes." Nick smiled. "We're taking a ride to a restaurant and it's a joy to be with you."

She smiled at the car.

Grand House was packed when they arrived.

Witkowski said to Tessa, "Let's go. I know another place only three blocks north of here."

"What's it called?"

"Fung's Kitchen. It's still on Classen. It used to be a fast food restaurant. They converted it to slow food."

Tessa giggled.

They were seated right away.

"I have to tell you, this is my first time here," Witkowski admitted.

"My first time, too."

"What did you want to ask me?"

The waiter showed up, set down two water glasses and gave them each a menu. He bowed and walked off.

Tessa took a sip of water.

"I want to ask how many cases are you on now?"

"I have three now but there is a fourth case I want to concentrate on in particular. It's not really my case but maybe I can keep the suspect in jail before he can do any more damage."

"Can you tell me what he did?"

"Yes, but it's nasty. You still want to hear?"

"I'm a big girl. I can handle it."

Before he answered he had no doubt that she could handle anything.

"This guy is stalking a young woman. She had been stalked and raped a month ago. That perpetrator is dead now." Taking a sip of water, he continued, "Right now this new stalker's in the county jail on unrelated charges."

"How dreadful."

Tessa watched him with her beautiful brown eyes. Nick noticed and felt warm. He picked up the menu. "Let's see what's for lunch."

Nick ordered an egg roll for his appetizer and Tessa ordered six fried Wonton. They made small talk while eating their appetizers. The waiter came back after they finished. Nick told Tessa to order her food first.

She said, "I'll have the deep-fried oyster with egg drop soup."

The waiter turned to Nick.

"I'll have the steamed oyster in shell with egg drop soup."

Both went for tea and water to drink.

"You like raw food?" Tessa asked.

"Sure, that way I get the full taste. But steamed isn't raw."

"Close enough for me." She sipped her tea.

"Well, how's your oyster?"

"It's very good." She smiled at him.

After they ate, they stayed and conversed comfortably for another half hour drinking tea. He had her talk mostly of her writings and journalistic career. He listened intently and asked questions. He felt his heart grow fonder for her with each passing moment.

She asked about his past and where he was from and what brought him to Oklahoma. He told her a very abbreviated story and left out the painful parts with Ruth. He explained that the marriage didn't work out.

Finally, she changed course and asked him questions for her paper. She seemed to flirt a little with him as she asked her questions. His self-confidence was always high, yet now it seemed to climb higher. Nick decided to tell her something about himself.

"I do have an antique telephone collection. I even have an 'I love Lucy' phone."

"You do." She excitedly said. "I *love* Lucy. Did she use that phone?"

Nick laughed. "No, that's what some people call it because they always had it on the shows."

"I'd love to see it."

"I think that can be arranged." Nick was beaming.

"So, do you have any children?"

"Nope. No kids. My ex-wife didn't want any. No pets either. She wasn't a pet person."

"Are you a pet person?" She grinned at him.

"I haven't really thought about it. Why, are you?"

Her long black hair framing her face made her look more like a model he thought.

As she observed him, she spoke in a guarded tone. "Yes, I am. The love of my life died seven months ago. His name was Lucky. He was hit by a car and I rescued him. Got him fixed up and had him for ten years."

Witkowski saw the sadness in her eyes and it pained him.

Witkowski said, "I'm sorry. I know people become attached to their pets."

"Yes, we people do," she said smiling.

He hesitated, then spoke, "Having a pet doesn't bother me. I like cats, dogs, and birds. I just never had one. I was an underprivileged child." He winked at her.

She slapped his arm. "Oh, phooey, detective. I doubt that you were ever underprivileged."

He laughed, then said, "Call me Nick."

"I remember you told me that when I first saw you, Nick."

He nodded then asked, "With your last name I assume you are of Italian descent?"

"Yes. I came over here with my parents when I was six. We settled in the Bronx for a few years. Then we moved to Buffalo and finally became legal citizens."

"So, how did you like Buffalo?"

"We visited Niagara Falls New York and the Falls in Ontario a lot, since Buffalo is close to the Canadian border."

"That it is and you didn't like Buffalo. So, what brought you here?"

"After college—I was taking journalism—I thought the wild west would be good for a new reporter to sink her teeth into writing for a major newspaper."

"Ah, I don't think *The Paseo* is a major newspaper. I'm not belittling you but I think your talents are wasted there."

"That's who would hire me at the time. I take it as learning the ropes."

Nick nodded. "That's good, but maybe I can put in a word at *The Daily Oklahoman.*"

"Oh, that would be great. I also want to write novels. Science fiction type."

"Your mom and dad still live in Buffalo?"

No. They live in Santa Fe now."

Witkowski saw that she had a far-away look so he said, "I came from a Polish background. There's a lot of us in Baltimore."

"You don't say," she giggled.

Nick laughed. "Yeah."

Tessa turned serious. "Do you believe in God?"

He was taken aback but recovered quickly.

"Yes, I do. I used to be Catholic but…" He looked sheepish, "I still believe in God."

Tessa looked at him sternly. "Once a Catholic, always a Catholic. Even a fallen away Catholic."

Nick felt, what, uncomfortable, defensive, ashamed? First time in his life that someone flustered him. He weakly said, "I assume you are Catholic?"

"Yes." She smiled. "I did stop going to church for a while."

He felt a little better and maybe braver.

"Oh? How come?"

"The Church left me. It changed…for the worse."

Witkowski knew he had to tread lightly but tread he would.

"What do you mean?"

"I won't explain it today. On another date I will." She smiled with twinkling eyes. "But I'll say this, I *am* going to church again because I found a true Catholic Church."

Nick became very intrigued now. He had finished eating a while ago and he pushed his plate aside. She did the same.

She continued, "It's now in a little chapel off of Britton Road."

"The Catholic Church is in one little chapel now? In Oklahoma?"

"Yes, but it's one of many Chapels and many churches in the country. Or for that matter, in the world."

Nick was stunned. He never knew that. Why hadn't he known? Then it came to him. Because he never sought it. He felt embarrassed.

"How is it, new, different?"

"No, it's the same as it has been for two thousand years. For some people it's known as Traditional Catholic. I'm the same but I call myself an orthodox Roman Catholic. That's orthodox with a small o."

"Well, I'll be a blue nose gopher, I didn't know they existed."

Tessa laughed. "Well mister gopher if you'd read the newspapers you might learn something."

"I might but I doubt it. Can't trust the papers."

"What or who do you trust?"

"You, Tess."

The waiter came over with the bill and Nick handed him his charge card. He thought, *saved by the waiter.*

After the transaction they stood to leave. She smiled at him and he smiled back. He felt great as they left the restaurant.

They looked at each other and Witkowski warmed up again. He went for her hand and guided her to the car. He opened the door for her. As he walked behind the car he said to himself in a muffled voice, "Nick, she's the one. Does she feel the same?"

He entered the car and they looked at each other. Then they laughed. Witkowski sure felt good. He turned on the ignition and drove back to headquarters. They didn't say much but Witkowski was comfortable in the silence.

When they got to Central, he walked her to her car and asked, "Will I see you again?"

She reached up and kissed his cheek. "Call me."

He stood there dumbfounded. When she started her car, he snapped out of it and asked her, "What's your phone number?"

Smiling up at him she said, "You're the detective." Then she drove off.

He watched her car recede into the distance. He figured she was around seventeen or eighteen years younger than he was. *Perfect*, he thought, *just perfect.*

32

Tuesday, August 8, 11:45 A.M.

Lance's phone rang. He hit the speaker button.

"Glitter Jewelry, Lance Pruitt, may I help you?"

"Lance, oh Lance." Tears and fear in the voice.

"What's wrong, Angie?"

"He's out. His sentence is over."

"Who, Chad?"

"Yes." More sobbing.

"Calm down, Angie. Where are you?"

"At work. He called here and asked for me. They knew it was him and told him I was in the restroom. Oh, Lance, I'm scared."

"Is he coming back to Cimarron Electric?"

"No. They fired him three weeks ago. While he was in jail. I'm afraid he'll be waiting for me outside."

"I'll let Ronnie off early and escort you home. She'll have her gun just in case."

"This is bad." She sobbed. "I'm a nervous wreck."

"Take some CBD hemp oil, try to relax. Ronnie will follow you home. She has a new cellular phone."

"I need more than marijuana. Get me some Xanax."

"That's not marijuana. I don't have Xanax. Try some Chamomile tea. It's soothing."

"Tea! I need you!"

"Angie, listen to me. It will be okay. I'll tell Ronnie if you all are followed, to call the police and head to the police station."

"Okay. She'll be waiting for me? I want to leave now."

"Yes, but wait 'til I call you back. I'll identify myself."

Lance hung up and went into the store. Ronnie didn't have any customers at the moment, so he motioned for her to come into the office. She had on a gray suit, pink blouse with a deep vee to show off the necklace better. Uh, huh. Whatever it takes.

"What's up, boss?"

"Would you be able to leave now and go to Angie's place of work and escort her home?"

"Sure. What's going on?"

"Chad Payne got out of jail today. Sure was peaceful with him locked up. But he's being his usual total pain in the ass self already. She'll wait for you. Make sure you have your gun. When you two get to the house stay inside until I get there."

He folded his hands on the desk. Slowly raising his eyes, stopping for a second at the cleavage, his eyes met hers and he said, "I'll pay you for the full day. The other two should be able to handle it. If not, I'll help. Concentrate on your surroundings and if you think you're being followed call Lieutenant Witkowski and go to the closest police station."

"Don't worry, I'll get her home safely."

"I know you will." He leaned back with his hands behind his head. "This guy is starting to cost me money and time. I have a feeling one day soon it will end, but at what cost? You know, Ronnie, what makes this world bad is people messing with other people who aren't even bothering them. A damn robber, thief or murderer bothers people who don't bother them. You have an idiot neighbor who wants to bother you for whatever reason his small mind comes up with. If everyone would mind their own business and take care of themselves this world would be a better place."

"Yes, I agree. I'd do this for no pay cause she's my friend."

"Thanks, Ronnie."

"No need to thank me. I wish the jerk would drop dead."

"I think he'll need a little help to do that."

After she left Lance decided to call Witkowski.

"Hey, Nick, that fool Chad Payne just got out of jail and he's already stalking and bothering Angie again." Lance could hear Witkowski letting his frustration go by blowing air into the receiver.

Lance started talking again, "He's a real asshole."

"Good, I'm looking for another asshole."

Lance laughed.

"I have other cases I'm working on. They're all assholes."

Lance chuckled. "Well I want this one locked up again."

"Okay Lance, I take it you're filing a complaint. Right?"

"Yes, sir."

"Okay. I'll write an affidavit for an arrest warrant and pick him up for stalking. I have to find a judge to sign it. It might take a while because most of them took off today or have court in another city. Let me check."

Lance heard a couple of clicks; the line went silent. Five minutes later Witkowski came back.

"I finally got ahold of Judge Mahoney's office. His sec says he's in court now but she will give him the message. I don't know when I'll see him but when I do if he likes what I wrote up and signs it, I'll get over to Payne's house and arrest him."

"Thank you, Nick. In the meantime, I'm suggesting to Angie to visit her sister in Baltimore."

"Good idea. Gives me a little breathing room. You know I work homicide and no homicide has been committed, so I'm doing this for Angie, on the side, half of it is on my time…as a favor."

"I appreciate that, Nick."

"Forget it, I want to do this."

They hung up.

Within half an hour, Ronnie arrived at the plant and Angie waited for her to pull up.

"Get in. I'll drive you to your car."

"Thanks. Did you see him?"

"No, but that doesn't mean anything. Park your car in a different spot every day."

"He's making my life a living hell."

"I hear you. That's why I'm here."

Angie pulled her car into the garage and Ronnie parked beside her. The garage door clanked down. Remotes are one of man's best inventions.

In the house Ronnie told her to pack some clothes.

"Why?"

"Because you're going to stay with Lance. I'll stay here.

"Does he know this?"

"He told me to tell you. He'll take you to work, or here, then drive you to work. I really don't know what he has in mind."

At six, Lance pulled into the driveway. Everything seemed okay.

"He hasn't shown up here," Ronnie informed him.

"Good." Turning to Angie, "Can you take a few days off from work?"

"Yes, I can take a couple of days. I already called to let them know."

"Okay. We'll take it day by day. You're not going to work tomorrow. We'll see how that goes. Leave your car here and I'll take you to my house. We'll leave at nine when it's kinda dark."

He placed his hands on his hips, looked up, contemplating.

"Ronnie, would you walk the neighborhood and see if his beat-up silver truck is out there?"

"Sure."

After fifteen minutes, Ronnie came back looking serious. "He's not out there, I'm pretty sure."

"Okay Angie, let's go. When you're in my truck lay down on the seat."

"I hate this."

"So do I."

As they reached I-40 Lance said, "So far, so good. You can get up now. I don't see him and no one seems to be following."

She lifted her head and said, "This is crazy. He made me leave my house."

"I know."

She let out a big yawn. "Sorry. I'm just so tired."

"You'll get rested at my house."

He left his truck on the driveway and opened the garage door. Inside sat the T-Bird and the Corvette. He took her by the hand into the garage then closed the door. He disarmed the alarm and unlocked the door to the house. Once in the house he turned on the driveway alarm. Leading her by the hand down the hall he showed her the bedroom she would use.

"Do you want something to eat or drink?"

"No. I think I'll just go to bed, okay?"

"Sure. The house doors will be locked and bolted. The alarm will be on, so things will be okay."

"Lance, I know this is my first time at your house, but I'd feel safer sleeping with you."

That caught Lance off guard. Still holding her hand, they walked into the master bedroom.

"I'm going to brush my teeth. Feel at home," Lance volunteered.

He came back to the bedroom and found her asleep, with her clothes on, on top of the bedspread. He covered her with a light blanket. Then he undressed and slipped under the covers into bed, turned out the lamp, and went to sleep. But it took him awhile.

33

Wednesday, August 9

Early in the morning Witkowski went to see Captain Richard Nelson.

"Hey, boss. Can I see you for a minute?"

"Sure, Nick, come in."

"I want to pick up Angie's alleged stalker this morning and bring him here and interrogate him. I told you about him before."

"Who? John something? I thought he was dead."

"He is. Angie's got a new stalker that's bothering her. Chad Payne."

"I remember now. I don't see a problem."

"Can I pull Phil Madsen off the street and take him as back-up? Give him some experience on pick-ups and interrogations."

"Let's see, he's interested in being a detective, right?"

"Yes, sir. He has a mindset that thinks like a detective should."

"Sure. I'll have the sergeant pull him. This way we can tell if he has the mindset. Maybe," he smiled.

"Thanks, boss. We'll leave as soon as he gets here."

"You want me to change into a suit?"

"Nah, you're good like that. I want a uniform with me. This guy is bad news and we might have a problem."

They crossed Colcord and entered the parking lot. They reached Nick's unmarked and opened the doors.

"Whew, it's hot. Leave the doors open a couple of minutes before we get in," Witkowski told Madsen.

After a few minutes Witkowski told Phil to drive.

"Chad Payne lives on the southwest side of the city. If he doesn't want to come with us, we'll have to persuade him," Nick said. He had researched his address through the OTC.

Madsen grinned. "No problem. We'll get him in the backseat comfortably."

"I'd like to keep him a couple of days. We might have to goad him. You alright with that?"

"You bet. Goading is a proper tool to get someone into an interrogation room. I think I read that somewhere."

Witkowski glanced over at him. Madsen was smiling. They were heading west on I-40 towards Yukon. They took Exit 137 to Czech Hall Rd. and headed south. When they came to S.W. 27th Street Madsen made a right.

They arrived at Payne's rental house and drove up the long gravel driveway at 411635 S.W. 27th, piled out of the vehicle and walked to the door.

"His silver truck is here. Got to be home," Witkowski said. "I was here the other day."

Madsen looked around and said, "This isn't a bad looking house."

"Cause it's a rental. Owners, probably keep it up to snuff." Witkowski had pulled the ownership records also.

Madsen looked around. "Not a bad looking area."

"Doesn't match the renter," Witkowski admitted. "I know he won't be happy to see me again."

Nick reached the door and gave a loud bang, bang, bang, with the side of his fist.

After thirty seconds of waiting, there was no response.

"Sure is slow getting to the door. Let me knock," Madsen offered.

The door swung open.

"Quit banging on the door!" Payne looked like he just woke up, wearing only light blue boxer shorts. "What the hell do you want."

"Police. We want to ask you a few questions."

"Again? What for? Let's see some I.D."

Witkowski said, "Cut the crap. You know me."

"Yeah. Wadda you want?"

Witkowski started to get angry but he stopped himself. Madsen swung his arms loosely at his sides.

"Put some clothes on. You're coming with us, downtown."

Witkowski shoved his way in surprising Payne, who let him in, with a mild, "Hey."

"I said get dressed."

Payne turned and went towards the bedroom, followed by Phil and Nick. He put Madsen in front of him just in case Payne got any crazy ideas.

When he finished dressing Payne stated, "Lemme call the dog in. He's out back. I don't want him out while I'm gone."

"Cute. You don't have a dog and you're not running today." Witkowski turned him towards the front door and pushed him.

"Hey."

Madsen escorted him to the car and Payne shrugged Phil's hand off his arm.

"I can walk myself."

Payne stopped at the car. Madsen opened the back door and Payne got in. Madsen closed the door, which automatically locked, yanked his door open, and jumped in the driver's seat. Witkowski strolled around the front of the vehicle and slid in. Phil then locked the front doors. Backseat passengers couldn't unlock their doors.

"I wanna call my lawyer." Payne said the magic words.

"You're not under arrest. Why do you think you need a lawyer?" Witkowski asked.

"I don't trust you guys."

Witkowski laughed. "You don't trust us? If we arrested you, you'd be in cuffs. So, how's that for trust?"

"I ain't saying nothin.'"

They drove the rest of the way in silence. When they arrived at Central, Witkowski led Payne by his right arm and Madsen had his left arm. Inside they took the elevator to the second floor. Payne was immediately led into one of the two interrogation rooms. Oklahoma City detectives don't cook their suspects. If Nick had something to finish before the interview, then Payne would have had to wait. Today, no waiting. Nick gave a heads up to one of the other detectives in the room to turn on the recording system when they entered the interrogation room.

Down the hall another detective waved at them as he went into the homicide room. Madsen gave him a mock salute and Witkowski nodded.

A table and three chairs sat in the room. Witkowski took one and pointed to the lone chair on the other side of the table. "Sit." After he closed the door Madsen sat next to Witkowski. Payne's chair back sat three feet from the beige painted wall. Nick and Phil sat with their backs facing the door. The doors of both interrogation rooms had no locks, the city considered them a fire hazard.

Witkowski pulled a card from his wallet. "I'm going to read you your rights."

"I thought you said I wasn't under arrest?"

"You're not. This is just to cover all bases. We're here just to talk," he misinformed Payne. He then read him his rights.

"You want a coke or coffee?" Witkowski offered.

"I'll take a cigarette."

"Can't. Not allowed anymore."

"Coke."

Witkowski looked at Phil.

"Would you please get Mr. Payne a coke?" Witkowski took the soft approach first.

Madsen got up and opened the door, went through and closed it.

"You know Angie Tilghman, right?" Witkowski wanted it recorded.

"Yeah. You know it."

"And what did I tell you about stalking Angie?"

"Look, I just got out of jail, so I ain't stalking that hoe."

Witkowski glared at him. "Don't you call her that again."

"Sure thing." He smirked.

Madsen came back in with the coke and handed it to Payne. He popped it opened and took a swig. Madsen sat.

"Don't play games with me. I've told you once and I'll tell you one last time. Stay away from her. If you are within five miles of her, I'll arrest you."

Payne laughed. "I'm scared." He took another drink. "You haven't got jack squat."

Nick looked at Madsen. The gloves came off. "Go turn off the sound and camera." This was pre-arranged with Madsen to shut down the recorders and guard the door so no one interrupts him. He got up and left again.

Witkowski waited a couple of minutes then he stood and walked to the side of the table.

Payne's eyes went wider than usual and he warily took a sip. Witkowski then stepped behind him. Phil should now be in front of the door, he guessed.

Payne appeared worried. He remembered the beat down by Witkowski at his house. "Whatchu gonna do?"

He barely got that out when Witkowski took his fists and boxed him in both ears. Payne let out a loud yelp. Nick grabbed the back of the chair, pulled it down, and jumped out of the way. Payne landed on his back. "Ow-wah!" The coke can in his hand went flying. Nick yanked him up.

"Pick the chair up and sit."

"You'll pay for this, shithead!" He sat while his right hand checked his ear.

Witkowski stood just off Chad's left shoulder. He formed both of his hands in a cup, inhaled deeply and connected behind Payne's head with sufficient force that brought his head down. His forehead and nose hit the table hard.

"Uh!"

Witkowski walked to the door and jerked it open. He surprised Madsen, who'd been standing guard.

Breathing hard Witkowski ordered, "Get some paper towels, Mr. Payne slipped and fell."

Madsen hurried off to the men's room.

Nick looked at Payne. He was moaning, holding his nose and forehead. Witkowski bent close to his ear.

"Do you understand me, now?"

Payne shook his head in the affirmative the best he could.

Madsen came in with the towels.

"He slipped on the coke he spilled."

Phil grinned at him and said, "Okay. Do we take him home now?"

"Yes. He's had a rough day."

Another detective peered in. "I heard some noise or something. Everything okay?"

"It's fine. He just slipped on some coke. We have to stop giving people coke."

Madsen took Payne by the left arm and led him out to the car. Chad had the paper towels up to his face all the way. Witkowski followed. He knew he walked a fine line legally with Payne.

After they dropped Payne at his house and were in the car again, Madsen said, "Dang, Nick, you busted him pretty good."

Witkowski smiled and looked over at Madsen. "Yeah. I think I finally made him a believer. That's what you gotta to do to get their attention."

"You scared me. You gotta be careful at Central and chill."

"You're probably right but he's a dirt bag."

"Maybe your girlfriend will mellow you out."

Witkowski smiled and thought of Tessa. "Yeah. Maybe she will"

***

Payne left his house and drove to a free clinic to get patched up. He used Witkowski's line and told them he slipped on spilled soda and smashed his face. An unfortunate accident. He would pay back Witkowski after his trip.

34

Friday, August 11, 2000 6:00 A.M.

Lance Pruitt took the Meridian Avenue exit from I-40 and headed south to the airport in light traffic.

"I'm nervous about flying," Angie Tilghman stated.

"This is a perfect day for it," Lance consoled her. "Hardly a cloud in the sky and no wind."

"I'm glad my sister said it was alright for me to stay with her for a while. I'm so tired of being afraid and looking over my shoulder."

"There's no way Chad boy knows you're going to Baltimore. You enjoy yourself. Take a day and go to the Inner Harbor. I'm sure your sister would like to be your guide."

"She did say something about going there and eating seafood. That'll be a change of pace for me."

"You'll love it."

"I wish you were going with me."

"Well, I was thinking that I'll be finished with my buying trip to Santa Fe in two days and maybe I could fly to Baltimore and meet you."

"That would be great." Angie smiled. Her love for Lance grew every day.

"Then I'll do it."

Lance slowed the Corvette as he approached the parking gate. He grabbed the ticket and the arm went up. He drove to the top parking lot and eased the car into a spot away from other cars. Mike Quinn and a friend were coming later to drive the Corvette to Mike's house. He wasn't leaving the 'Vette at the airport. Never know what could happen.

As they walked to the terminal the sun warmed their skins and Angie warmed his mind and heart.

***

"Delta flight 787 is now boarding to Atlanta and Baltimore," The intercom announced. "Flight 787 is on schedule to depart at seven-oh-five."

Lance and Angie stood.

"I'll miss you," she said.

"Me, too."

They hugged, then kissed.

"I love you, Angie."

He watched her walk down the jetway ramp and waved to her as she turned the corner. Sighing, he picked a good spot at the window to watch her plane take off. He still had time before his flight took off at 7:20.

A man walked to the ticket counter. The attendant looked up, saw the bandages, started for a second, then said, "May I help you?"

"When's the next flight to Baltimore?"

"Tomorrow morning at seven-oh-five, layover in Atlanta."

He glanced at his watch, 7:10. "Nothing sooner?"

"No sir."

"Okay, I'll take one ticket to Baltimore."

"And your name sir."

"Chad Payne."

After getting out of jail the morning of August 3, Payne had stayed in his house waiting for a call from an acquaintance of his at Cimarron Electric. Angie had informed a co-worker about taking two weeks off to go to Baltimore. After Witkowski's beat down on him two days ago, he left his house and stayed at a motel near the airport. This morning the wait paid off. His informant called him at the motel and said she would be leaving this morning.

"You owe me bigtime for this, man."

Payne smiled as he said, "No problem. When I get back, I'll give you two thousand dollars. You earned it."

"Great."

Payne thought, *you fool.*

He knew his way around Baltimore having lived there until age 22 when he had to split because the cops were after him. He had murdered a prostitute after having sex, because she was a prostitute. Both acts, the killing and the sex, satisfied his warped sexual appetite. The reward, sex, for his needs and the punishment, killing, for her being a woman.

A month later he committed more murders and had to leave Baltimore quickly. This would be his first time back since 1976.

People glanced at his nose strip and the bandage taped on the swollen cut on his forehead from Witkowski. It was still painful. Regardless, he felt safe here. The little bastard wasn't at the airport, and nothing would stop him now. His plans were that after he killed Angie he would come back for Witkowski and ambush him. The thought made him feel giddy.

"Final boarding call for American flight 337 to Albuquerque."

Lance checked his watch: 7:13. He rose and moved with the line, gave his pass to the attendant. As she checked it, his eye caught a man walking from the Delta gate.

Seconds later she said, "Here's your pass, sir."

"Thank you." He took the pass and strolled toward the jetway entrance. Before he entered he took a look over his shoulder and studied the man as he turned a corner. He wondered what happened to him. His forehead and nose were bandaged. The guy wore a ball cap and sun glasses, dressed in shirt and slacks and he kept staring at Pruitt. Probably nothing, though Lance's anxiety level rose.

Payne had spotted Pruitt as he walked by. In his impromptu disguise, Pruitt didn't recognize him. He smiled as Pruitt turned the corner.

***

At a few minutes after noon Cathy Mason spotted Angie coming through the doors from the jetway. She rushed up to her. "Angie, you look good," Cathy complimented.

"Thanks, sis. So do you. I'm so happy I'm here."

"Tell me your problem."

"I will, but let's get out of here first."

On the way to Cathy's car Angie asked how her husband, Peter, was doing.

"He's doing great. Just got a promotion to office manager. He's away this weekend for a convention in Seattle. He'll be back Monday, late afternoon."

"I guess he likes his work as a stockbroker."

"Oh, yes. He likes helping folks make money. He's also a financial advisor."

Angie thought, yeah right. More like separating their money into his pockets. She couldn't help herself; she didn't like him.

"How long has he been with Legg Mason?"

"Six years now. They've been around since eighteen ninety-nine."

"So, I guess you're here to stay."

"You bet. This is their headquarters."

On their way to her car Cathy informed her sister that Peter Mason was a blood relative of Raymond A. Mason.

"He is?" Angie sounded impressed.

"Yes, and Ray started the company in 1962 at Newport News Virginia. It later merged and became Legg Mason, joining the company founded in 1899."

"You seem to know a lot about him."

"Oh yes. He's really impressive. And the headquarters stayed in Baltimore and now it's located at 100 Light Street with forty stories, the tallest building in the city."

After hearing some more history of the company Angie realized there wasn't any chance of her sister ever moving back to Oklahoma. She felt saddened as they reached Cathy's car.

They left Baltimore-Washington International airport and took I-195W to hook-up with I-695N, the Baltimore Beltway, and proceeded north to Towson.

Along the way, Angie told her sister the sordid details of Chad Payne. She still felt uneasy as if something evil followed her. But, if she wasn't safe with her sister, where would she be safe? Her throat went dry and the saliva was hard to swallow.

"Does this city still stink, Cathy?"

"It doesn't really smell here on the west side. They cleaned it up a bit."

Shortly, Angie closed her eyes for the rest of the trip.

***

At nine A.M. Witkowski had called Lance.

"Lance, this is Nick. Is Angie going to Baltimore?"

"She's in the air as we speak."

"Good. I have a warrant now but couldn't serve it yesterday because Payne wasn't home and evidently hasn't been back. I talked to some neighbors and they saw him leave yesterday very early in the morning. So, no arrest yet. I'll try again later today, but I think he's in the wind."

Lance didn't like that. "Okay. I'm on a buying trip to Santa Fe. I'll be back in a couple of days. So, I guess it's no rush."

"Like I said, I'll try again today. I'll keep doing it 'till I arrest him," he emphasized.

"Okay. Thanks again."

"There is a BOLO out for him so I hope we get him soon."

"That would be good. Nick, I really like Angie."

"She'd be good for you."

They hung up.

35

Towson, Maryland
Saturday, August 12, 2000

Chad had laid low and slept at Will Rogers until he could board his flight today. He was asked once by security if he needed anything, a subtle way of checking him out. He told him he was waiting for his flight and showed the man his ticket. Security said he could stretch out on a padded bench in a darkened alcove. Chad thanked him. He thought with his bandages the man felt empathy for him. *The jerk.*

"Welcome to Baltimore-Washington International. It is now twelve-oh-two P.M. Eastern Time. The temperature is 89, overcast and high humidity. Please keep your seatbelts on until the plane has come to a complete stop. Thank you for flying Delta."

Chad strolled briskly through the terminal and picked up his one piece of luggage. The Skycap hailed a cab for him. He told him thanks with a dollar, got in the cab and said, "Days Inn in Towson."

"What is address?" asked the Pakistani driver.

"It's on Loch Raven Boulevard, Baltimore." *Don't they have any Americans driving cabs anymore?*

From the Baltimore Beltway the cabbie took exit 29B and drove south on Lock Raven Boulevard. The motel sat just beyond the underpass of the Beltway.

Payne checked into his room, threw his suitcase on the bed, and closed the drapes. Going over to the suitcase he opened it and took out a hollowed-out book. Getting it passed the security point was no problem. He hoped nothing would ever happen to change that.

Opening the box, he lifted the Beretta Cheetah model 84. He stroked the .380 and shut his eyes savoring the oily smell of gun cleaner. Payne cleaned his guns often, once or twice a day, even when they were not dirty.

"Baby, I have a job for you."

He laid the weapon down carefully and retrieved a piece of paper out of his suitcase. Cathy's address had been written on it. Checking Angie's mailbox every day paid off. He knew from the return address on a letter it was her sister. Angie told him a couple of times about her younger sister, Cathy from Towson, Maryland. Close to his original stomping grounds.

That bitch thought she was going to dump him for that rich bastard. He'd kill her before he'd let her go to someone else.

He looked at his digital watch: 1:20. He put a light jacket over his tee shirt and stuffed the pistol in the right pocket.

Payne picked up the phone and called Enterprise car rental and had them deliver a Ford to him. He drove the rental to the Beltway and headed west. Three minutes later he took the York Road exit 27 and drove north. A minute later he turned right on Evans Avenue, then made a left onto Stevens Lane. Cathy lived in one of the smaller older homes. He slowed the car, scanning for the right number, 2007.

"There it is."

He parked the Ford and twisted out. Looking left and right to make sure no one was watching. He reached the door and knocked. No one answered. As he knocked again he tried the door knob—locked. Payne wrote on his lawyer's business card and shoved the card in the jam, walked back to the car and drove off.

Ten minutes later Cathy and Angie came home.

"Somebody left a card," Cathy said. She read it. "Oh, no."

"What's the matter, Cathy?"

Angie grabbed the card. *I'm coming.* "How did he…" She started to sob.

Cathy took Angie's hand and said, "Quick, let's get into the house."

With Angie stumbling and crying, Cathy struggled with the packages as she helped Angie from falling. Cathy slammed the door and dropped the packages on the soft beige carpet. She guided Angie to the bedroom.

"Lie down and I'll fix you some ginger tea," Cathy said.

Cathy returned four minutes later and set the cup on the nightstand.

Angie sat up, drank some tea, then stirred it with the tea bag.

"Where is your friend, Lance?" Cathy asked.

"He's in Santa Fe."

"Can we get in touch with him?"

"If he has his mobile phone with him, we can."

"Give me his number, I'll call."

Cathy had to walk while she punched the buttons on her portable. She couldn't sit, if she did she'd have to join Angie, and have some tea. That would slow her down. One of them had to take charge and Angie seemed too hysterical.

"This is Lance."

"Oh, thank God you answered."

"Who is this?"

"Cathy, Angie's sister. Lance, Chad is here."

"What! There with you now?"

"No. In Towson someplace, I think. He was at the house here when we were gone. He left a note. It said, I'm coming."

"So am I. It's lunch time now, I'll be there as quick as I can. Stay at the house. I have your address. Bye."

Lance cussed, "That S.O.B. He's not going to stop."

Lance closed his jewelry case and said to his seller, "Sorry, Henry, I've gotta go." He rushed out the door, ending his buying trip.

"Be careful." Sixty-year-old Henry Gibson hoped for the best. To himself: "That boy gets into more situations than anyone I know."

Once in his rental car and on the road, Lance called Witkowski's direct number. He was glad he paid extra for the expanded coverage on his cell.

"Witkowski. Homicide."

"Nick, this is Lance. Angie has a situation in Baltimore. Chad is there."

"Oh for crap sake. How'd he get there? Never mind. Dumb question. Why is he there?"

"To bother Angie. She's in Towson with her sister. What should she do before I get there?"

"What do you mean before you get there?"

"Well…she needs help now."

"My advice is to stay put and have her call the Baltimore County police. Let them take care of it."

"I'll tell her."

"As you know now, I couldn't serve Payne the papers. That mutt never came home. Now I know why. I have new info on him. He is one bad dude. Stay away from him."

"We want to, but he won't leave us, her alone."

"Then hop a plane back here, tell her to fly back. I'll meet youze guys at the airport. He'll follow her and I'll pick him up there."

"I'll try," Lance responded, "I have to get to her in time."

"I thought my talk with him would cool his heels," Witkowski said. He had hoped for the best. Guys like that don't cool down, they lay low. "Wait a minute, wait a minute, you're not flying to Baltimore. You have her come here."

"She's scared, she wants me to come, so I *will* go."

Nick knew he couldn't force him not to go. "Look man, for the record, I think you should come back here. And Angie flies back here. I'll grab him at the airport."

"Sorry, Nick, no can do. She needs me."

Nobody saw that Witkowski rolled his eyes. Then he said, "I can't make you stay. But remember this, Payne is a psycho. Stay away from him."

"We'll try."

Feeling defeated, Witkowski said, "Keep me informed."

"I will."

Lance then called Cathy's house.

"Cathy, this is Lance. I might not make it in time to do anything, so my friend, a police lieutenant told me to tell you to call the Baltimore County police."

"Okay."

***

August 12

Late that night Payne drove into Baltimore by taking the beltway. It was a short drive to the York Road exit. This time on York Road he kept going south until it changed to Greenmount Avenue. He came to a light and had to stop. The cross street was East 39 Street. The light changed and he began looking to his left for East 38 Street. He found it and made the left turn. This area of Baltimore appeared worse than he remembered. He checked his watch: 11:34. He cruised down the one-way street until he reached Old York Road. He spotted a black man, a homeboy, caddy-corner to him, standing in front of a corner bar. He made a left onto Old York Road, a one-way road, and pulled up to him. Payne powered down his passenger window.

"Hey man, got any dimes?"

The man eyed him warily, "What dat?"

Must have been used to being asked that since he began walking towards the car.

"I ain't no cop. I want some good, and I mean good, crack."

"Okay, man, I got some good shit. Go up the street to da trees."

Payne did as told—driving three hundred feet and pulled over to the curb. There were a couple of dim street lights that struggled to cut the darkness.

The man caught up and quickly came to the driver's window. He handed the rock in a small baggie over to Chad. As he put the money in homeboy's hand, the man grabbed Payne's left hand and at the same time had a knife to his throat.

"Give me rest of yo' money, cracker."

"Sure. Take it all. Take it easy with that knife. I'm getting it."

With his right-hand Payne reached into his jacket pocket, pointed the Beretta up, and fired through the jacket. The bullet struck homeboy in the throat. Chad drove off as the man fell to his knees in the street holding his shattered windpipe.

"Son-of a-bitching nigger."

Payne was close to the intersection and saw that the traffic light was green. He stepped on the gas and came to the traffic light in one second and made a left onto East 39 Street. He saw the light turn green as he approached the intersection at Greenmount, slowed his speed and turned right, heading north again driving toward his motel. Payne constantly checked his mirrors for any signs of trouble.

"I should be okay, those assholes in that hood are probably used to any ruckus."

Good fortune travelled with him; traffic was light and every signal he approached was green. He reached the motel and pulled into a spot. The key card made a light click and he went in. He closed the door, slid the chain and turned the bolt. He turned on the bathroom light only. As he sat on the threadbare chair he retrieved the rock from his pocket. The bureau drawer creaked when he lifted the pipe out. Opening his pocket knife, he cut off a piece and dropped it into his pipe. The match hissed. Payne was on his way to turmoil.

36

August 12

"Mike, do you have time to go with me to Baltimore?"

"Baltimore? Why?"

"Angie's in trouble. Chad followed her there."

"How'd he know she's there?"

"Don't know. Not important now."

"Damn. I've got some vacation time I can take. Where are you?"

"Santa Fe, but if you're coming I'll fly into Oklahoma City and we'll fly out together. The trip will be on me, of course."

"Hell, yes, I'll go. Not because the trip is free. Angie is still my friend and I'll help you save her, if that's what we're doing."

"That's it. I think this might get nasty. Are you still in?"

"I'm scared already that I might get hurt again but I'm in."

"Good man. I'll meet you at the airport in seven hours."

"Seven hours. How come so long?"

"I said I was in Santa Fe. I have to drive to Albuquerque to catch the plane. Then there's a layover in Houston. I'll see you in seven hours."

"I'll be there."

"Thanks buddy."

Lance ended the call. He was already heading toward Albuquerque on I-25. His mind raced as fast as the car. Pruitt wouldn't and couldn't count on the police. He had to get to Angie in time. He had to.

***

The police told them to keep their doors locked and to call them if Chad came. Then they left.

"That did us a lot of good," Cathy said facetiously.

Angie rose from the bed and started pacing the floor. She stopped. "Call Ronnie, she's at my house. What time is it?"

"Two. So, it's one in Oklahoma."

"She'll be there. Call her, please."

"What'll I say?"

"Give me the phone when she answers."

The wood floor creaked as Cathy walked into the dining room and picked up the portable phone. A bead of sweat ran from Angie's temple to her jaw and dropped.

"Hello."

"Ronnie, this is Cathy. Angie wants to talk to you. Hold on."

Cathy walked back to the bedroom and handed the phone to Angie.

"Ronnie, I need you here. Can you come?"

"Angie. What's the matter? You sound awful."

"Chad is here in Towson. Lance is coming but it will take him awhile. You can be here sooner. I'll have Lance pay for it. The police will come if I have to call them. But then it will be too late."

"I'll go to the airport now. In the meantime, you and Cathy stay in the house. Make sure to call the cops if you have to. You hear?"

"I will," she replied grudgingly.

They hung up and Angie slowly went back to bed. She felt like a sitting duck and she didn't like it.

***

Ronnie Tanner had always been lucky and today was no exception. She had been able to book a rare Saturday afternoon flight for 3:15 central time, with Southwestern. She had to change planes at Atlanta's Hartsfield, arriving at 6:03 eastern time. She took off again at 6:30 eastern time and arrived at Baltimore Washington International at 8:14 eastern time. She hailed a cab that took her to Cathy's in thirty minutes.

***

Aug. 12, 9:15 P.M. ET

Cathy Mason spied the cab and saw Ronnie get out. Before Ronnie reached the door, Cathy flung it open.

"Come in quick," she commanded.

"Where's Angie?" Ronnie's eyes swept the living room.

"She's in the bedroom lying down. You sure made good time."

"Got lucky with the flight and had the cabbie speeding for extra bucks. Yeah, less than six hours since the call ain't bad. Had to change planes in Atlanta."

Ronnie dropped her carry all at her feet.

"Does Lance have the keys to your house?

"No. Why?"

"Cause we're leaving. Leave him a note and tell him we'll be at his friend's house; Jim, I think his name is. If Chad breaks in and reads the note he won't know where it is. By the way, do you?"

They made their way upstairs to the bedroom.

"Yes, Angie told me the address before her nap. How do you know about his friend?"

"I called Lance on the way to the airport and he told me what to do."

She walked towards Angie.

"Angie, wake up, dear. It's Ronnie."

Angie's eyes fluttered open. She smiled and opened her arms to receive Ronnie's embrace.

"Thank you for coming. You're such a good friend."

"We've got to get out of here. Let's go." Cathy said. "I'm taking the longer way to Jim's in case your stalker is following. If we need to run back here, I'll take the short cut."

Cathy got into her Dodge Stratus and Angie entered the back seat. Ronnie rode shotgun. The garage door made a racket riding the rails to the top. Cathy backed out slowly. Ronnie looked in all directions for anything suspicious. The Dodge picked up speed as they drove down the street.

"Well lookie here. Are you girls trying to leave ol' Chad behind?" Payne started the rental and pulled out.

Cathy drove south on York Road, glancing in the rear-view mirrors occasionally. She turned left at Seminary Avenue then turned left onto Kings Road and found McClaren's house just past the York Manor Swim Club. His two-story house sat on the corner.

Chad had followed and parked four houses away. He got another business card and wrote the house number; 1612. Then he pocketed it. He slid low in the seat. With a monocular to his eye he spotted Angie.

"You beautiful bitch, you're mine and no one will have you."

Cathy walked to the door with Angie behind her. Ronnie positioned herself behind Angie looking up and down the street. A flash of light caught her eye. It came from a Ford, but she dismissed it as the reflection off the mirror. Wait. The mirror faced the other way, so it couldn't be a mirror. Jim opened the door.

"Come in ladies."

When they were safely in he locked and bolted the door.

"Tell me what's happening."

***

Sunday, August 13, 12:45 A.M.

Lance hailed a cab as he and Mike left Baltimore-Washington International terminal. As they sped off, Lance gave the cabbie Cathy's address. Their cabbie took the same route as Ronnie's cab.

"I think Ronnie should be at Cathy's now." Lance said to Mike. "It will take us around thirty-five minutes before we get there."

Mike grunted and kept looking out the window.

After ten minutes Mike broke the silence. "Shouldn't you call Angie and let them know where we are?"

"They know we're on the way."

"I got a bad feeling. Suppose something is wrong?"

"Mike, it's all wrong. We shouldn't even be doing this, but some A-hole has other ideas."

They were quiet the rest of the way, thinking their private thoughts.

***

1:14 A.M.

Lance and Mike arrived at Cathy's house twenty-eight minutes after leaving the airport. The women had left ten minutes earlier. Lance paid the cab driver. They walked up to the door and saw the note.

"They went to my friend's Jim's house. Must be trouble, I told them to go if necessary."

"Did you notice our ride's gone?" Mike asked looking down the street.

Lance took out his cell phone, found that he was in the carrier's area so he pressed the numbers for Enterprise rental. In thirty-five minutes, they were finally on their way to Jim's. Mike had been fidgety; wasted time.

"I told them to stay put at first, but I think it's okay to go to Jim's." Lance was second guessing himself and hoped he would be validated by Mike.

Mike said, "Somebody thought it was a good idea and maybe it is. If they thought the jerk was lurking around, they would take off. We wasted time waiting for this car."

Lance ignored the remark. "I just hope Chad didn't follow them. That sucker is sneakier than a Gypsy."

Lance tapped the steering wheel to a non-existing tune. "When we get there keep your eyes open."

***

1:45 A.M.

Jim opened the door. "Come in buddy." They embraced in a bear hug, slapping each other on the back. Lance introduced Mike.

"Jim used to work for me ten years ago until he saved up enough money to buy his own store in Towson," Lance told everyone.

Jim drawled, "Yeah, there's more money to be made here."

"Fleecing the rich," Lance joked.

They laughed.

"Four years ago, I took a month's vacation here and Jim showed me the sites in and around Baltimore. He's a great host."

"Well, well, the gang's all here," Chad said. He had been parked a couple of houses down, on the other side of the street, watching and waiting for the right time to grab Angie. He'd have to wait a little longer.

Jim McClaren stood five feet nine inches and slim as Lance remembered. His thinning hair was still black.

"I see you're still losing your hair, Jim."

"Hey, what do expect, I'm thirty-six years old."

"That's a reason for losing hair? Huh, after tonight you might lose it all."

"Okay, give me the lowdown, pardner."

"I hear you haven't lost your western accent." Lance winked at Angie. She sidled next to him. They put their arms around each other.

"We are having trouble with an ex-boyfriend of hers. He doesn't want to let go. This guy is also violent and he's here now in the Towson area. Somehow, he followed her here. I'd like you to put her up until we can get her back to Oklahoma City."

"Damn. Sure can do, Pard. Do you or your friends have any weapons?"

"No. We thought it best not to tweak the tiger's tail here in this state. What have you got?"

"I have a Smith & Wesson Model 19, a .357 magnum and a Model 10, .38 special. Both four-inch barrels. And a couple of rifles."

"I'll take the .357. Give Ronnie the .38., she knows how to handle it."

Jim went to the gun safe and opened it. He left the two long guns alone and handed Lance a .357 and a speed loader. He held out the .38 to Ronnie, also with a speed loader. Then he passed out the ammo, twelve rounds each of .38 Specials.

Jim looked at them soberly. "I'm keeping the magnum ammo."

"That's okay. These will do nicely," Pruitt said.

Jim reiterated, "You know, in this state, we don't have a concealed carry law. Only the bad guys can run around with guns on them. And I bet your guy has one with him."

"Oh, I bet he does. But I'd rather be tried by twelve than carried by six," Pruitt said.

"Crooks love this state. We get them from Virginia and other states that let their citizens protect themselves," Jim said locking his safe. "Now we have your crook from Oklahoma."

"Sorry about that," Lance said. Then Lance whispered into Jim's ear, "He may die in Maryland."

Jim turned away. "I don't want to hear it. I didn't hear a thing."

Lance turned to Cathy. "I think you'll be safe at your house but keep your eyes open." To Ronnie: "I'm glad you're here. Would you stay here with Angie?"

"Of course."

Turning to Jim, Lance asked, "Is that okay?"

"You bet, pardner."

"Mike and I will get a nearby motel. All of you have my mobile number. I'll get you on the earliest flight out of here, Angie."

Lance went to Angie, hugged her again and kissed her.

"You'll be alright here for the night."

Turning to Jim. "Take good care of them."

"You know I will, Pard."

Payne saw Cathy leave first, and alone. Lance and Mike left a few minutes later. He waited a half hour.

"Looks like the others are staying." He patted the Beretta. "Show time, baby."

Payne started the car and pulled into Jim's driveway. There were no fences around the house or any of the other houses. The houses were not sitting close to each other. At least fifty feet separated the houses.

He left the car, strolled to the house and went around to the back. Payne pulled a lock pick from his pocket and opened the door in one minute. It was not dead bolted. Their voices floated to him from the front of the house. His Beretta lead him to the voices. He slowly peeked around the corner in the kitchen. He saw them at the end of the hall, in the living room, seated in different spots. Angie faced him, and the others had their backs to him. He entered the living room and Angie screamed.

"Hi baby," he growled, looking grotesque with his swollen face and bandages.

Gasping, Ronnie twisted around and pointed the .38 at him. He fired first. She dropped the gun and grabbed her left shoulder. The bullet pushed Ronnie

Tanner back against a chair; a red stain spread down her arm. She slouched in the chair as shock overcame her. Screaming, Angie ran upstairs.

Jim struggled out of his overstuffed chair and was stunned by two shots from Payne's gun. He dropped back into the chair, hit in the upper left thigh and left side.

Payne ran up the stairs and found Angie in a locked bathroom. He reared his right leg back and smashed the door into large splinters. He grabbed pieces of the door and fought his way in. Angie stood in the tub screaming, "Get out! Get out!"

With his left hand he grabbed her by the hair and led her down the stairs.

"Get off! Get off, you jerk!"

"We're gonna take a little ride to the reservoir. When we get outside don't make a sound or you're dead."

Angie nearly fainted when she saw Ronnie and Jim. Ronnie held her arm looking pale and crying silently. Jim held his hands on the wound in his thigh, grimacing.

Payne glared at Jim and Ronnie, pointing his pistol at them. "I should kill your friends, but I like to live dangerously." His laugh sounded insane to her. Then he threatened them, "If you call the cops I'll come back and kill you both."

Angie walked on rubber legs to the car. He shoved her in. Then he tore off down the street.

Jim felt the burn of the bullets as he crawled to the telephone and pulled on the cord. The land line phone hit the floor with the sound of bells. He stretched for the receiver and struggled to punch Lance's number. He didn't care about Payne's threat, he hoped he could get Lance.

"This is Lance."

"He's got her," Jim's voice sounded weak.

"Jim is that you?"

"He's taking her to…," Jim coughed.

"Where, Jim? What happened?"

"Reservoir, reservoir. Lance, help." His voice weaker now.

"Hang on, buddy, I'll send help."

Lance clicked off.

"Come on Mike. The bastard got Angie."

As they ran to the car Lance gave Mike the phone.

"Call 911 and get them over to Jim's house. The bastard's taking her to Loch Raven Reservoir. He has to be taking Dulaney Valley Road."

"Quiet while I call."

Lance fired up the car and flew down the road. Mike gave the 911 dispatcher the details as he knew them.

When Mike disconnected, Lance said, "There are very few places Chad can park, so it should be easy to spot the car. Look for the unusual."

The headlights of the car danced on the trees. In the dark they made no impression on Lance or Mike, even with the sparse street lights. They continued driving and came to the dam. The dam area had more lights. Lance drove across it.

"Damn!"

"We just crossed over it," Mike said.

"Shit, then. The road forks. See."

Lance pulled quickly to the side.

Mike strained to see in the ambient light. The headlights and dim street lights were useless. If the lights went out you wouldn't see your hand in front of your face.

Lance explained, "I don't know how well he knows the area. The left fork is Jarrettsville Pike and it leads to some lonely spots. Dulaney Valley Road continues right and it also has lonely spots."

It began to rain, slowly at first. Seconds later it picked up speed. Lance turned on the wipers then pounded his fist on the steering wheel.

Mike asked, "What else is on Dulaney Valley?"

"I think there is a golf course."

"And Jarrettsville Pike?"

"Nothing that I know of. Some houses, few and far between."

Mike fingered his Fu-Manchu mustache. Lance hit the dashboard. After a minute, Mike said, "I have a hunch we should take Jarrettsville Pike."

"Let's go then. Forty years ago this place used to be packed with teenagers and young adults. Good thing cars are absent now but keep your eyes peeled. It's going to be hard to see them in the dark and rain, even with these dim street lamps. And the trees make it twice as hard to see."

A half mile later rounding a curve, in between two spread out lamp posts, their lights flashed on the taillights of a Ford. They saw it parked facing into the trees. The telltale e was on the trunk.

"That's got to be it," Mike said.

They squeezed next to the rental's driver door. Lance checked the time on the dash clock: 2:00 A.M. He turned off the ignition then gave Mike a small flashlight, the only one he carried with him. Mike looked at him quizzically.

"At least it's not a penlight," Lance whispered.

Quietly they left the car. Putting his finger to his lips, Lance motioned to Mike to check the rental. The .357 came out of Lance's waistband. The distinctive click told Mike the hammer was cocked. Mike shone the flashlight into the car. For a small flashlight, it had a strong beam.

Mike shook his head that no one was in the car. Lance let the hammer down slow. A scream startled them.

"Where'd that scream come from?" Mike asked.

"I can't tell."

The throbbing in his ears from his heart beating made it hard for Lance to hear. He looked at Mike, his face wet with rain, perspiration and adrenaline. He thought Mike's face appeared pale through the faint light. He took the flashlight from Mike.

Mike broke the silence. "Man, this is like a real forest."

They heard a loud moan.

"This way," Lance said.

They charged a few feet through the trees, briers and brambles, the flashlight bouncing its light all over the place. Then immediately the ground sloped downward. The rain started to fall harder. A flash of lightning and two seconds later a loud crack of thunder. It sounded like a gunshot and they moved faster. A tree root grabbed Mike and he fell. Lance caught himself slipping and slowed. He cautiously approached a small clearing. Payne's large Magnum flashlight lay on the ground pointing at the couple. It was enough light to see what was going on. He saw Angie on the wet ground with Chad bending over her. His left hand poised to strike her face. His right hand with the gun pressed on the space between the neck and shoulder.

"Stop!"

Payne whirled around shocked. He held his Beretta away from them at an angle. Realizing this he made an effort to correct his error. But Pruitt had been quicker.

"With your left hand throw the gun towards me. Slowly!"

After a few seconds hesitating, Payne dropped the weapon to his feet. He had a snarl.

"Hands up! Turn around! Drop to your knees!"

Payne did not turn around. He slowly lowered himself on one knee, then the other.

Pruitt didn't challenge Payne for not turning around. "Now move away from her!"

Chad walked on his knees toward Lance, with an evil grin locked on his face. The bandage had fallen off his forehead making his features more grotesque.

"Lay face down with your arms out, palms up."

He laid down on the soaked ground. It seemed he didn't care, he was already drenched.

"Palms up, asshole! Angie move to me." Again, Payne didn't obey.

Angie first crawled then tried to stand but too close to Payne. With lightning speed he rolled towards her. Grabbing her he held her tightly, rolling until she was on top of him, face up. She struggled to free herself but he held tight. His legs wrapped around hers and his left arm across her throat. With his right hand he took out a pocketknife from his back pocket. He opened it with his teeth and held it to her throat. It happened so fast that it caught Lance off guard. He moved the .357 up and down and back and forth. He couldn't shoot. He might hit Angie.

A flash of lightning and an immediate clap of thunder didn't slow Payne down.

"Throw the gun to me, prick, or I'll stick her!"

Lance hesitated.

"Now shithead!"

Pruitt did as he was told. Payne got up with Angie. Lance could see a red spot on her neck.

Quinn had been watching from the trees where he stayed hidden from Payne. As soon as Payne bent down with Angie, to retrieve the gun, Mike made his move.

The noise stunned Payne for a second and he looked in the direction of the sound. Mike flew through the air at him. It was a perfect hit. All three went down. Lance ran slipping towards them and jumped into the fray reaching for the knife. Angie fought to get out from underneath. Mike pounded Payne's face. Lance had both hands around Payne's wrist. Lance almost lost his grip because his hands were slick from the rain. Angie finally scrambled away. Payne kneed Lance in the groin. He still hung on. Mike's pounding started to take its toll on Payne's ability to fight. But Mike was also getting tired and so was Lance. Payne felt his chance. With the strength left in him, Payne's arm broke free and slashed Lance across the chest. Pruitt fell back into some bushes. Payne then stabbed Mike in the side as he rolled away from Payne. Chad Payne jumped up and looked around for the gun. He found it in Angie's hand. She pointed the .357 at him. Pruitt watched, frozen, then he looked for Payne's Beretta.

"Hey, baby, give me the gun," Payne urged. He noticed the hammer was cocked and nervously licked his lips. He wiped mud and water from his eyes with his dirty left sleeve. He slowly walked towards her.

Angie held the revolver with both adrenaline-fueled hands, shaking. He cautiously kept moving toward her. Resolved she knew what she would do. Her head was soaked and water ran down her forehead, into her eyes. She had to keep blinking. She stood her ground, breathing hard. In a bright flash of lightning she saw his sneer plainly. He was six feet away.

"Give me the gun, bitch."

"Okay." Her face contorted with hatred. "Bullets first."

The sound and muzzle flash startled her and she didn't hear the thud as the bullet found its target. Payne stumbled back and collapsed. Angie carefully walked over to him. He looked up at her.

"I love you, baby."

A crack of thunder.

Still holding the gun with both hands, she cocked the hammer with her thumbs and pulled the trigger.

Angie's two shots had hit him in the upper chest. He was still alive looking at her trying to say something. From his mouth nothing came out but bubbles in a froth of blood—his lungs had been shredded. She stared down at him. He coughed emitting a strange sound that confirmed he was dying. Blood quickly filled his lungs and soon he would drown. He tried to raise his arm. Angie still had the gun pointed at him. Again, using both thumbs she pulled back the hammer.

Lightning flashed brilliantly giving Angie a clear target. Payne had an evil grin.

Mike could only watch as he lay on the ground holding his side. Lance was thirty feet away and started to move towards her. He was half way there when the gun exploded. At the same time an ear-splitting thunder clap overwhelmed them. Angie didn't stop and cocked the hammer quickly three more times. All the slugs found their mark at center mass.

The adrenaline rush had overwhelmed her and she stood there, shaking and crying, as the thunder diminished and rolled away from them.

37

August 13, 2:35 A.M.

Before he reached Angie, Lance found the Beretta. Pulling out his shirt he bent over and with the shirt picked up the gun. He carried it over to Payne's body and dropped it next to him. Then he went to Angie. He took the .357 from her and shoved it into his waistband. Pulling her against him, they hugged.

"It's over now, babe."

They held each other as she sobbed, the rain mixing with her tears. A few seconds later the rain slowed down.

Mike called out, "Hey guys, I'm still alive."

"Sorry Mike. Are you hurt?"

"Yeah. He stabbed me in the side. It doesn't feel too good."

"Let's get you to a hospital. St. Joseph's isn't too far from here."

"Is he dead?" Mike asked.

"He's dead, buddy." Pruitt walked to where Payne laid.

"What are we going to do with him?"

"Leave his ass here to rot," Angie said between sobs. She took her hand to wipe away the tears and managed to smear a little mud under her eyes.

Lance looked at her, then said, "After we get patched up I'll call the police anonymously." He stared at Payne. "On second thought let someone else find him. When the police find out he is a no-good piece of shit, hopefully they'll put him on the back burner."

Lance stood still, observing the corpse, thinking. He reached in his back pocket and pulled out a small notepad. He found his pen in his right pocket. It had snapped in half, probably during the scuffle. He took the bent refill out and pocketed the rest of the broken pen. On the pad he printed badly:

Get my prints and check the Maryland juvenile records.

With his right hand, Pruitt lifted his shirt and tore the page out using the shirt. He knelt beside the body and still using the shirt, stuffed the paper into Payne's pants pocket. Being that close to Payne's smelly dead body made him queasy.

No vehicles passed by as Lance checked the road. Angie, still sniffling, and Mike in pain, helped each other walk slowly back to the car. Then Lance cleaned up the area the best he could so no traces would lead to them. With his foot he scooted the Beretta against Payne's body, then wiped the muddy trail marks with a branch and took the branch with him. He took Payne's knife—less blood evidence against them.

They were waiting for him at the car. Lance ripped Mike's shirt off and wadded it and had Mike hold it tight against the knife wound. Angie helped Lance to get Mike into the seat comfortably. She took over pressing the shirt against his side and held it there. It was sprinkling, then two minutes later it stopped. Lance started the car, turned the lights on and left the crime scene.

Later a brief cloudburst totally obliterated the crime scene.

***

August 13, 3:30 A.M.

At the hospital, the doctor patched Mike first, then Lance. Fortunately, no vital organs were involved and the wounds weren't too deep for either of them. The Doc told them that after they got home, Mike would have to be bedridden for a week. The nurses asked how it happened and looked with skepticism at their story—karate practice with real weapons, an accident. The nurse told them it must have been some practice; blood and mud. She wrote it down on their records anyway. Lance figured the cops would be looking for people with guns, not knives. He paid in cash which raised a few eyebrows, but they were happy to get the money from out of state people.

All of them took the elevator up to the ICU floor to check on Jim and Ronnie.

"How are they doing?" Angie asked, fully recovered from her crying but her eyes were swollen.

The nurse scanned them. "Are you relatives?"

"Friends." Lance spoke first.

"They are pretty bad off, critical, but they should make it. Who should I tell them who asked about them?"

Lance spoke up. "Tell them Tom, Dick, and Mary stopped by."

"Well, Tom, the police were trying to get answers from your friends, but we had to shoo them away. Do you know what happened?"

Lance spoke again for them. "No. We just heard they were here at this hospital."

"News travels fast, I'd say," the nurse pointed out.

"Quark said in the near future it will be even faster," Lance said. "Almost with lightning speed. Like instantaneous."

"Who's Quark?" Nurse "Ratchet" asked.

"Another friend." Lance smiled.

In the parking lot Mike asked, "Why did you give them phony names?"

"They're not phony names, they're real." Lance grinned.

"You know what I mean."

"Because this socialist state doesn't give out conceal carry licenses. We would be the bad guys. You're not allowed to defend yourself."

Turning to Angie he said, "Let's go to your sister's house and get the hell out of here, in case the nurses wise up or start caring." He thought maybe he should give the police a heads up on Payne. "I think I'll call the cops at Cathy's house, then we get moving."

Halfway to Cathy Mason's house, Lance changed his mind again and stopped at a payphone. He dialed 911.

"Baltimore County, Precinct six, what is your emergency?"

"There's a dead man at Loch Raven Reservoir off of Jarrettsville Pike."

"Where exactly?"

"You'll find him."

"How did you find him?"

"I was hiking."

"Your name, please."

Smiling, Lance hung up. He lifted his shirttail and grabbed the receiver, wiped it down, and put it back.

They were exhausted when they arrived at Cathy's.

"Angie, you poor thing." Her sister hugged her.

Lance said, "We're leaving for the airport in a couple of hours. Would you help Angie pack?"

***

August 13, 5:05 A.M.

After they left for the airport, they first stopped by Jim's house. Pruitt had wiped down Jim's .357 and left it in the car. Then he wrote a note saying: I'll get you another one. He placed the note where Jim would find it. As Lance got back into the car he told Angie, "Wipe the blood and prints off Payne's knife."

They took a longer way to the airport by driving east on the beltway then south to the Francis Scott Key Bridge. Lance wanted to make sure the evidence would never be found.

As they were crossing the Key Bridge, Pruitt slowed the car to thirty. They were at the highest point on the bridge, one hundred and eighty-five feet. He opened the car window and the fish smell blew in. Cathy let them have a pair of old work gloves. Angie took the gun by the barrel and flung it as hard as she could. A perfect throw. At that height, no one would hear the splash. Then Angie grabbed the knife by the blade and flicked it out the window. The few cars were far away but gaining on them, so Lance sped up. They had plenty of time for the 6:30 A.M. connecting flight to Atlanta.

Chance was with them again, they had three seats together.

Once airborne, Lance asked Angie, "How are you doing, babe?"

"Okay. I'm glad it's over. I feel relieved one way but upset another."

"It's not an easy thing to take someone's life."

"That's the scary part. I loved it. At least doing it to him."

"It's okay. As some cops say about killers, NHI—no human involved. You don't have to feel bad about getting rid of scumbags. It was either you or him. I'm glad it wasn't you."

"Me, too. But I feel bad that Ronnie and your friend got hurt. My fault."

"No, it's not your fault. It was that jerk, Chad. His fault."

Angie yawned. "Okay, if you say so."

"I do." Now Lance yawned.

They held hands and tilted their heads towards each other and closed their eyes. Sleep overtook them quickly.

38

Oklahoma City

Monday, August 14, 2:00 P.M.

Witkowski's old phone rang.

"Lieutenant Witkowski, Homicide."

"Hey, Nick, this is John Smith, with Baltimore City Police."

"Yeah, hi, John. What's up?"

"You know how news spreads like wildfire among the precincts."

"Yes, it happens here too."

"You gonna love this but last night Baltimore County 911 gets an anonymous call saying there was a dead body at Loch Raven Reservoir off Jarrettsville Pike. A lieutenant detective, Richard Frey, goes to check it out with his men and they find the stiff, shot six times. Sounds like maybe a revolver. They're checking that now. A Berretta next to him. They checked the magazine, to see if it was full. It wasn't, three rounds might be missing. No brass around. No clues who did it. Before they got there, we had a thunderstorm, lotsa rain. Place was wiped clean anyway. Stiff is middle age white guy. The M.E. was checking his pockets for I.D. and this is what you're gonna love, his name is Chad Payne, your guy."

"Wait. You found Payne at Loch Raven?" *Had Payne kidnapped Angie?* "I thought he might be back here now, in Oklahoma."

"Nope, he's here, and that ain't all. The M.E. found a note in his pocket, no prints on it, and it said, 'Get my prints and check the Maryland juvenile records.' So they did. You could have knocked me over with a feather."

"Okay, they checked the juvie with the prints, and…"

"Old cold case. Remember that shootout you had in nineteen seventy-six?"

"I remember all too well. We never did find him."

"Well a killer did. Chad Payne is William Brocius, the killer who shot youze guys."

Witkowski was speechless, a lump growing in his throat. Seconds later tears started to form. He rubbed his eyes. Elation, relief, justice, sadness, anger, and other mixed emotions flooded into his mind.

"Nick, are you there?"

"Hold on a sec," Nick said hoarsely.

"Sure man. Take your time."

Forty-five seconds later Witkowski spoke softly, "Are you still there?"

"I'm here. One other thing. Baltimore County is not going to pursue the killers or killer, and neither are we. Baltimore City is closing that case, too. Anyway, they are probably long gone. I think he got what he deserved. If I find out who it was, I'll give him a medal."

"I think I will too. Thank you very much, John. You made my year."

"My pleasure, Nick, it made ours too. The em eff got what he deserved."

"Will you send me a copy of the report. I mean everything."

"You got it, as soon as we finish it."

"Thanks, John."

"Don't mention it. So long."

Witkowski said bye to a dial tone. He hung up, went around his desk and closed the door and locked it. He stood there for a couple of minutes thinking about his fellow officers and friends. He still missed them after twenty-four years. He walked back to his desk and put his head down on his arms and silently wept. Just a minute later he lifted his head and with a hankie he wiped his eyes. He then smiled and took a deep breath. "Maryland got the scumbag killer back. Born there, died there," he said to no one.

Witkowski then called his friend Joe Mantegna. After two rings he answered: "Hello."

"Joe, this is Nick."

"Witty, you ol' buzzard. Haven't heard from you in a few months. Hope this is a social call," he said laughing.

"Better. This is a celebration call."

Laughing, Mantegna said, "You didn't get Tessa pregnant?"

"Heck, no. Better. Remember the shootout in 1976 when I came close to buying the farm?"

"Oh, yeah."

"Well that killer is dead."

"You serious?"

Witkowski told him the whole story. He ended it with, "I never got him but he was got."

"Damn, Witty. And the powers don't know about your friends."

"No. So mum's the word."

"I wouldn't tell them shit anyway."

Changing the direction of the conversation Witkowski said, "So, how's retirement?"

They bantered a few more minutes and hung up. Next, he called Pruitt and told him the happy story, except for Payne's real name.

"I didn't tell Angie or Mike that the jerko had a juvenile delinquent record or that he was from Baltimore," Lance informed Nick.

"Good. The less anyone knows the better. Do *not* say anything. Like what happened, how it happened, why it happened, or anything else. And *I* don't want to know. You've told me too much already. I will say, off the record, I'm extremely glad Payne is dead and gone. Baltimore City police are ecstatic." Witkowski chuckled.

"Okay, Nick. Mum's the word."

"Good. Mum's getting around." He chuckled. "Just for the record, the note they found on Payne had no prints or anything. Like I told you earlier they couldn't find any evidence. The place was cleaned. Which means neither I nor the Baltimore City police or Baltimore County have any idea who killed Payne and we are not going to pursue it. That being said, I'd like to say that was a good trip and I'm happy Angie is safe. I want to buy youze guys lunch soon."

"I understand. Sounds great."

"But, if I had known everything about Payne, I wouldn't have let ya'll mess with him. I would have taken care of it a long time ago. I had him and let him go...again. Talk to you later," Nick said and hung up.

Witkowski wished he had pulled the trigger but this seemed like poetic justice. Killed by a frail, untrained woman. Justice was served. In his mind he could see the S.O.B. stoking the fires with Cunningham, with encouragement from a pitchfork. He felt better and chuckled again. Armed civilians caught, killed him and sent him to Hades. He would never tell that story. Witkowski would always tell people the truth, that he nor the police ever caught the guy who killed his brothers and wounded him in nineteen seventy-six. He would never say his name, William Brocius. Whenever he told the story it would always be "a killer" that had gotten away. It was his dark secret. He knew he shouldn't feel like that. Witkowski wanted to forget him, but he never would.

Witkowski went to see Captain Richard Nelson and told him the news. Together Captain Nelson and Nick went to the Police Chief, Jack Towne, and told him the written report they wrote up. The chief decided then to get a team together and search Brocius' house.

After the meeting with the chief, Nelson and Witkowski walked back to Nelson's office.

"Have a seat, Nick."

Once seated Captain Nelson asked who Nick wanted on the team. In deference to the history that Witkowski had with Brocius/Payne, he got to choose his men. This would be Witkowski's scene.

"Well, Cap, first I want Art Morgan, since it's his area and he knows about the two stalkers. Then I want Phil Madsen, and the new man, Feterman. I forgot his first name."

"Thomas. Likes to go by Tommy."

"Okay."

"You sure about him? He's fresh out of the Academy."

"He seems really sharp to me. He's got to learn sometime. I'll pull him off his beat."

"Who else?"

"That's it except for T.I."

Nelson smiled. "That's a given. Three forensic people should be enough. You said it was a small house."

"Yes. Easy to turn upside down."

"You want to do it today or tomorrow?"

"Now. Today. The sooner the better."

The captain looked at the wall clock: 3:15.

"Okay. Round 'em up, head 'em out," he ordered.

Witkowski stood, mock saluted, and left. He smiled all the way to his office to call the troops.

They all stopped at Braum's on Council Road and Reno Avenue for a quick bite. There was still plenty of daylight left. They arrived at the house at 5:10. Art Morgan drove his plain wrapper first onto Brocius /Payne's driveway. Nick pulled his plain wrapper Ford behind Art's. Phil Madsen and Tommy Feterman got out. Nick propelled himself out at the same time. The T.I. person parked the white Dodge Crime Scene truck behind Nick's unmarked. The other two forensic persons drew near to the back of the truck in their car. Everyone gathered on the long front lawn around Witkowski.

"Alright people, I want every nook and cranny checked for anything and everything. Phil and Tommy, search for items. Every creep like this mutt has trophies. Find them.

"Forensic, dust for prints, check for blood, etcetera. You know the drill."

They entered the house and Nick remembered how he saw it the first time. It looked the same. Forensic spread out and went to doors, window sills, lamp tables, pulled out their kits and started the dusting process. Another began taking pictures.

Phil and Tommy began to check the rooms and closets. Nick looked around and thought.

Madsen busied himself yanking off bed sheets and flipping mattresses. Then he pulled out some drawers dumped, what little was in them, on the mattress. Feterman looked through a closet taking clothes out, dropped them on the floor and stepped on them trying to feel if anything was in the pockets. Finding nothing he went into a smaller bedroom with a table and a chair. He smelled gun oil. Opening the closet door, he saw five rifles standing against the back wall. On the shelf he saw pistols, revolvers and the ammo to go with everything. Feterman whistled to himself.

"Lieutenant! In here. Weapons."

Witkowski limped at double time to get there. He arrived and cried, "Holy crap! Don't touch anything." He turned and yelled for Bob, the lead forensic man.

Everyone wore paper booties, coveralls and snap on gloves but Witkowski still reminded them, "Take the weapons out singly and be careful. We don't know if any are loaded."

"Lieutenant!" Madsen this time. "In the kitchen!"

Witkowski made his way arriving to find Phil kneeling, with his head and upper body in a bottom cabinet. A shoe box next to him. "What-cha got?" Witkowski asked.

Madsen pulled out another shoe box. "Photos in that box." He opened the one in his hands. "More photos. Dang. These must be his trophies."

Nick looked down. "Yes, they are. Put them in the car. We'll go through them at Central."

He grabbed his cell phone and called Nelson.

"Cap, we found a plethora of weapons and photos."

"Anything good?"

"Yeah. Looks like they are his victims. We'll call the other cities and ask about any unsolved cases and missing persons."

"I'm sure they have some. Good work, Nick. When do you think you'll be back?"

"Sometime late, Cap."

***

Tuesday, August 15, 2000

In the morning Pruitt was late getting to his store at Pennsylvania Avenue. He reached his desk and sat behind it. He looked at his watch, 10:10. He leaned forward in his chair and reached for the phone. He called Gary Smith.

"Hello, Gary. This is Lance Pruitt."

"How are you doing, man?"

"I'm fine, thanks. Are you still interested in buying my stores?"

"Does gold glitter, do diamonds sparkle? Hell yes, all three of them."

"Great. Would you want to come down here to the Penn store with your lawyers and papers at six?"

"Today? Let me see." Silence. "I've checked everyone's schedule and six p.m. would be fine."

"That works. Bring your checkbook while I'm still weak."

"Will do. Thanks."

"Oh, one other thing. Also included are the employees and especially Ronnie Tanner."

"Uh, well…"

"They are all great employees and I'll vouch for them one-hundred percent."

"Okay. Deal."

Lance gingerly set the receiver back on the cradle. His stomach felt tense and queasy. He was going through with it. He was selling his babies. He bought the first store twenty years ago. But it was a good deal for him, though he always felt like this, whether he was buying or selling. Pruitt planned to take some time off and relax. He knew he deserved it. Only one person could help him relax.

Pruitt looked at the office door when he heard a light knock. He watched as it opened and Angie Tilghman walked in. They smiled at each other. Lance reached out his hand.

Acknowledgments

Thank you, Master Sergeant Gary Knight of the Oklahoma City Police Department, for the information I needed to make the story realistic. My special thanks to Jane Hirsch for her encouragement, comments, and catching small important errors. Author Terry Hubbard, thank you for all of your help catching those pesky mistakes and making this a better novel. Many thanks to Eric Lueb, who enhanced this novel immensely, with his great eagle eyes, and made this novel flow smoother. Thanks to Jean Reed, writer and author, for her insightful, hardline criticism of some of my ideas that would not work. Any mistakes, embellishments, artistic license are solely my responsibility in this work of fiction.

www.ingramcontent.com/pod-product-compliance
Lightning Source LLC
Chambersburg PA
CBHW061059100726
47911CB00012B/311